IT SEEMED TO HAVE A MIND OF ITS OWN . . .

"Welcome aboard the KNIGHT 2000."

"Thank you. What is all this? It looks like Darth Vader's bathroom."

"This is a one of a kind car, Michael. It is faster and safer, and stronger than any machine in the world. It is completely fuel-efficient and is entirely operated by microprocessors which make it physically impossible for it to be involved in any kind of collision or mishap, unless specifically ordered by its pilot."

"Pilot? Don't tell me this thing flies."

"No. But it thinks."

KNIGHT RIDER

KNIGHT RIDER

GLEN A. LARSON and ROGER HILL

*Based on the Universal Television Series
"Knight Rider"
Created and Written by Glen A. Larson*

PINNACLE BOOKS NEW YORK

KNIGHT RIDER

Copyright © 1983 by MCA Publishing, a Division of MCA Communications, Inc.

An original Pinnacle Books edition, published for the first time anywhere.

First printing, November 1983

ISBN: 0-523-42170-2

Can. ISBN: 0-523-43160-0

Printed in the United States of America

PINNACLE BOOKS, INC.
1430 Broadway
New York, New York 10018

9 8 7 6 5 4 3 2 1

For

MICK GARRIS

friend, ally, and dynamite lunch companion

KNIGHT RIDER

ABOUT THE AUTHOR

Among Roger Hill's varied pursuits is the calling of film historian, which has led him to the statement that he "was made the same year as John Huston's *The African Queen*." Born in Fort Worth, Texas, and educated at the University of Iowa, Hill has worked as a journalist for major daily newspapers in Las Vegas, Seattle and Chicago. Since 1977 he has made his home in Studio City, California, and his other interests include music criticism, cartooning, photography, raising Alsatian show dogs and "hunting for decent Chinese food." This is his fourth novel.

1

Thirty-five people held their breath, while the high roller at the head of the crap table challenged fate and the odds one more impossible time.

Tens of thousands of dollars were down on the green felt before them all.

This was that rarest of happenings—a "gentleman's game"—playing itself out amid the din of wins and losses, the clinking of cocktail tumblers and the monotone judgments of dealers, pit bosses and croupiers. All around them were noisy tourists temporarily fat with paychecks and savings, but the denizens of this particular crap table in this particular Reno gaming house were not dressed like tourists. And respectfully, they kept silent during play.

The backbeat of the music thumping vigorously out of the casino's lounge was a physical stimulus, urging players to win through sheer body English. Combined with the action at the tables, it made the blood pound and brought sweat to the palms and temples of the more nervous gamblers.

The high roller was not nervous.

Dressed in a conservatively cut white dinner jacket, he had not even bothered to loosen the impeccable knot in his tie through an unprecedented eighteen straight passes at the crap table. Fully two-thirds of the wagerers gathered around his table had no idea who he was. They shook their heads in amazement and swore his streak could not last—and then pushed ever-larger bets out onto the playing field anyway. Others at the table knew that here was a distinguished man of ability and competence, and they were a bit less nervous about offering up their bets to his skill. And a small elite among the group could identify the man as Charles Acton, head of the multinational Consolidated Chemical Corporation, a man whose personal wealth could only be estimated in the high eight figures. The men in their tuxedos saw Acton as a role model and symbol of capitalistic success; the women in their costly DeLancé and Dicristefano gowns saw him as a reserved, paternal power broker, a man with impressive character lines weathering his face and just the right touch of iron gray tinting his sideburns and temples. Everyone was clearly impressed, in awe or cowed—and so kept quiet while Acton, the high roller, rolled one more time, tossing the large casino dice from behind a teetering pyramid of yellow-and-black hundred-dollar chips.

Acton did not rattle the dice overmuch, or pray to the gods or blow into his hand for luck. He did not even afford his female companion for the evening a glance while he threw. He was not a superstitious man, and applied his characteristic concentration to the game at hand. He rolled again, and all eyes followed the flight of the speckled cubes.

They bounced against the far wall of the crap table as per regulation, and tumbled to rest displaying four and three—a natural seven.

"Seven, the winner," said the croupier, getting tired of repeating himself.

A roar of approval rose from the thirty-five bettors, and as fresh racks of chips were broken and disbursed Acton turned and smiled at his companion, displaying no overt excitement at his nineteenth win in a row.

"I can't seem to lose tonight, Tanya," he said.

Tanya Walker's eyes were on the hundred-dollar chips—bumblebee checks, in casino parlance—as they accumulated in front of Acton. The croupier's rake had to make five trips before the win was paid off.

She linked her arm through Acton's and with gentle pressure pulled him close enough to speak confidentially. "Don't say that. It could lead to bad luck, and that's—"

"I don't believe in luck," Acton cut in with a smile as the dice were once again pushed his way.

Tanya was a tall, striking woman, with a body that was the essence of breeding, bone structure and exercise. She made the other women at the table look cheap and tawdry, and this privately pleased her. When the men in tuxedos were not watching the dice in Acton's fist, they were eyeing her—her magnificent honey-blond hair, her aristocratic manner, her calculated motions, her desirable body. There was a hint of arrogance in her eyes and at the corners of her mouth. She was not Acton's lady-of-the-evening; this was clear to everyone at the table. Acton had not given her the slim fox stole she wore, or the emeralds and silver that adorned her. Acton had not given her the thin, elegant wristwatch with the precise diamond workings, the watch she checked again as soon as Acton turned his attention back toward the game.

Some people at the table even thought that Tanya might be some sort of elegant bodyguard for the corporate overlord. They would not have been far wrong.

The bettors watched Charles Acton, and Tanya Walker watched Fred Wilson.

Wilson, Consolidated's husky security chief, was stationed across the casino. She picked out his close-fitting three-piece "power suit" near the action over at the roulette table, where he stood apparently watching the turn of the wheel. He attracted no undue attention— casinos were accustomed to people just standing and watching, either afraid to take a plunge except by proxy, or recording numbers and balancing odds in their heads until they felt secure enough to step up and put their money where their eyes had been. Wilson returned Tanya's attention with an almost imperceptible nod.

Nonchalantly, he raised his hand to adjust the volume wheel on the flesh-colored hearing-aid stationed in his right ear. A flesh-toned wire trailed back into his styled hair, down into his shirt collar and around to the booster unit clipped to his belt beneath his suit jacket. As his fingertip brushed his ear he spoke into the tiny speaker grille concealed in the closure of his own watchband.

The roulette wheel in front of him came up on a house number, and the players groaned as their bets were collected. House numbers busted everyone.

"Okay, Lonnie," Wilson said softly. The electronics supplied by Consolidated Chemicals were state-of-the-art; he did not have to raise his voice. "Acton's winning big. He's tied up at the table. It's now or never. Do it."

Wilson drifted back a few paces, and observers drawn to the roulette wheel moved around him. His new vantage allowed him to see the bank of elevator doors on the far side of the casino, just in time to watch a statuesque, willowy brunette in a low-cut, blue evening sheath step into the next available upward-bound car. He wondered idly just where Lonnie managed to hide the power pack for her own radio in a dress that left nothing to the imagination. Probably high up on a garter belt, beyond the slit in the dress, most likely.

The elevator doors closed and Wilson moved back to the roulette wheel's periphery.

Wilson was not aware that he himself was being observed, from one of the casino's three free-standing bars that infiltrated the gaming floor proper like little islands.

Sitting behind a mostly untouched straight glass of ginger ale was a younger man, rugged, rangy, in his mid-thirties, with finely chisled features, stark blue eyes and a healthy storm of dark curly hair. The bar mistress had winked slyly when delivering his drink, and he had winked back with a smile that, if it were to be applied to the gaming tables, would charm the chips right out of the racks. But now all his attention was on Wilson, and Lonnie, who had just stepped into the elevator.

Another cheer went up from across the floor. Action had won again.

The handsome young man at the bar opened his black leather jacket and touched a finger to a microswitch inside his belt buckle, an enormous oval of hammered silver.

"Muntzy? I think it's coming down. Wilson just sent Lonnie into the elevator. You copy?"

The voice of Muntzy, his partner, answered from his post on the twelfth floor of the casino hotel, ringing tinnily in the young man's own earpiece: *"Copy loud and clear, Lieutenant. If she shows up here, I'll have a front-row seat for the whole sting."*

Lieutenant Michael Long felt a butterfly of

anticipation tickle his stomach. Six solid months of cat-and-mouse investigation into possible illegal hijinks within Consolidated Chemical Corporation might come to a head in the next few moments. Evidence implicated Charles Acton's own security chief, the man now standing near the roulette wheel. Michael decided that to try to alert Acton himself would be fruitless, perhaps even dangerous. Let the man enjoy himself. He left his transceiver open. His personal mike was hidden behind an American flag pin on the lapel of his jacket.

"I've got her, Mike—she just went into Acton's suite."

"Be careful," Michael said into the tiny metal flag.

"Hey, junior, I've got ten years of experience on you. I'm the original man of steel. You're the one I'm worried about—you're right in the middle of the snake pit."

"Thanks, Daddy," Michael said sarcastically. Muntzy was a good partner, a good backup man.

He knew that like the most professional of thieves, Lonnie would have a key to Acton's suite, Number 1214. She would know the combination of the safe inside the suite's big bedroom closet—a standard-issue safe sunk into the rear wall, the type casinos routinely installed for the private use of their highest rollers. As safes went, they were fairly secure— with stainless-steel faces and interior hinges, rooted inside a lot of concrete and moly-tungsten, and crawling with burglar alarms. All of which were rendered impotent by the combination, which Lonnie was sure to know. Outright theft was unlikely. The best possibility was that Lonnie would slip in, photograph the contents of Acton's safe with a microcamera set on speed-snap, and slip out. Theft of industrial secrets was the new piracy.

Acton came up a winner again, and the chips piled up anew. Michael glanced down at his watch. Lonnie had entered Acton's suite ninety seconds ago. He waited.

Upstairs on the twelfth floor, Muntzy did likewise. He was disguised as a hotel handyman, with coveralls and a clanking beltful of equipment. No problem hiding *his* radio patch, but he had that most demanding of police jobs—surveillance, the ability to wait and wait and do nothing until everything jelled. He had stationed himself in the corridor between the elevators and Room 1214, blocking the hallway with a maintenance ladder and changing the fluorescent tubes inside a ceiling panel for the benefit of passersby. He had idly changed the same tube nearly two dozen times when Lonnie finally showed up. Attractive woman, Muntzy thought as she passed him, her body moving fluidly inside the sheer evening gown. She tossed him a fleeting, polite little smile. He smiled back and continued fiddling with the disengaged light until she vanished into the suite.

Downstairs, Michael noticed that Tanya Walker seemed totally oblivious to Acton's latest win. Several times she glanced up toward Wilson. Did she suspect him as well?

Michael saw Wilson's hand drift up toward his ear again.

Lonnie's voice sounded in Wilson's receiver: *"Finished."*

Again Wilson spoke discreetly into his watchband. "Batten it down and get the hell out of there. Be sure nobody sees you." She had accomplished her job fast, but not fast enough for Wilson, who was a stickler for efficiency.

"We're clear. There's nobody in the corridor but an electrician—"

Wilson's heart jumped and his body stiffened, but he kept his cool, hissing into his mike. *"Electrician? You didn't say anything about an electrician!"*

"He works for the hotel, Fred. Don't worry. I've seen him around before. He's just an electrician. We flirt."

Wilson's fists closed tightly. "Stay put in the room." At the crap table, Acton was gathering huge mounds of checks into his arms.

"Stay? For how lo—"

Wilson cut Lonnie off and hurried across the casino, toward Acton and Tayna Walker.

Michael hustled off his stool and beat Wilson over to the table. Acton's face expressed happy satisfaction.

"Come on, Wilson," Acton said. "Time to call it a night."

Wilson's eyes met Tanya's briefly over Acton's shoulder. "But Mr. Acton, you're on a roll."

"I got to be chairman of Consolidated Chemical by knowing when to quit winners," Acton said with the stern admonishing tone of a lesson giver. He turned to Tanya. "Let's go, darling. Be sure that our security stays in tow until we get our winnings into the room safe." When Acton mentioned security, he nodded toward Michael Long, who was politely pushing through the press of gamblers on the opposite side of the table. Then he moved past Wilson, bound for the cashier's cages.

"Delay him," Wilson whispered to Tanya as she passed. Then he caught Michael by the arm as he moved to catch up. "Stay close to Mr. Acton, Lieutenant. My boss is packing a lot of money."

Michael could not yet tip his hand and let Wilson know he was aware of his involvement. And to contradict Wilson now would attract attention in the wrong direction. As it was, he afforded Wilson a curt nod and hurried to catch up with Acton and Tayna.

"Move it, Lonnie," Wilson transmitted. "Get out of there *now*. Acton's on his way up."

Lonnie, who had the suite door cracked and was now regarding the electrician in the corridor suspiciously, said: *"What about the guy on the ladder?"* Nervous sweat broke across her brow.

"Forget him. If he follows you, I'll take care of him. Just get to your car and head east, out of town, to the rendezvous. We'll pick up the film from you there. Now *move it!*"

Wilson ducked away from the crap table

just in time to avoid being spotted by Michael, who cast a frantic glance back over his shoulder to keep tabs on the security chief. Michael stayed close to Acton—he had to stick with the money.

Upstairs, Lonnie pulled the door to Room 1214 shut and moved briskly past Muntzy toward the elevators. They did not trade cordial smiles.

When the lift doors slid shut Muntzy transmitted: *"She just left, Lieutenant—in a big hurry."*

"I know," Michael said, still trailing behind Acton and Tanya. "They just broke ranks down here. Wilson put me in charge; that's means they've got a broken play. I just lost him. Can you stick with Lonnie?"

"Back me up if I blow it!"

"I'll be right behind you, Muntzy. We've got six months of work about to pay off at three-to-one."

Muntzy stripped off his utility belt and let it clatter to the floor. Deciding against the elevator, he made for the access door to the hotel stairs.

As Tanya and Acton watched the cashiers convert the bumblebee checks into easier-to-carry banded stacks of greenbacks, Michael saw Lonnie leave the number-two elevator, her long, lithe legs moving in and out of her gown, her billows of dark hair fluttering behind her in her haste to leave the casino.

A moment later, Muntzy burst through the push-bar door from the stairwell. My god, thought Michael, proud of his partner—forty-four years old and he humps along in pursuit faster than most rookies.

Muntzy's voice came over the ear link: *"Relax, Mike. I've got her in my sights."*

"Careful, Muntzy—I still haven't gotten Wilson back in mine." Michael scanned the press of bodies in the casino again and came up empty.

He just missed Wilson's three-piece suit, easing into the corridor near the elevators. Wilson hurriedly transmitted: "Gray. Do you read me? They've made Lonnie; she's grown a tail. Guy in a maintenance suit. Burn him!"

A cold, reptilian voice came back over Wilson's receiver. *"I've got her,"* it said, totally flat and devoid of emotion. After a beat, it added, *"And I've got him."*

Michael's eyes fixed on Wilson, near the elevators. Quickly he signaled a pair of hotel security guards, who rushed over. "Stick with Mr. Acton; don't let him out of your sight."

Acton turned from the cashier's window. "Lieutenant Long, what—?"

"Please, Mr. Acton, wait right here—don't leave these cages or guards for an instant!" He shoved away from the group and legged it toward the elevators. Wilson was already gone.

Acton looked after him. "What's he talking about?" he said to Tanya. "Where is he going?"

"Michael!" Tanya called in his wake. *"Michael!"* Flustered, she turned back to Acton. "I don't know what's gotten into him, Charles.

I'll get him. Be right back." Then she, too, was off.

Acton started to call after her but gave up. He shook his head and gave the security guards an exasperated shrug.

Michael rounded the corner near the elevators. At the opposite end of the corridor, two glass exit doors wafted shut on silent hydraulic closures. He ran full-out down the hallway. "Muntzy! *Muntzy!*" he said breathlessly into his mike. "Look sharp! I think Wilson made you, and he just left the casino!" After getting no response in his ear link, he shouted, startling the idlers in the hallway. *"Muntzy!"*

The twin doors crashed backward as Michael burst outside. Sitting at a taxicab turn-in was a sedan bearing the gray and gold Consolidated Chemical security staff logo. Wilson was just slamming the passenger door. The sedan lurched away in a wheel-squealing rush and evaporated into the traffic.

The casino doors had not yet closed when Tanya dashed out and spotted Michael making tracks toward his own car, a jet-black, pantherlike street machine parked in the security lot. She shucked her fur stole to the pavement and chased after him, making excellent time despite the precarious heels on her shoes.

"Michael!"

She caught up with him just as he found Muntzy slumped against the side of his car, still clutching the door handle. His free hand was trying to contain a rapidly widening swatch of fresh blood staining the midriff of his electrician's coverall. "Tres Piedras ..." he grunted, then coughed.

"Muntzy!" Michael dropped to one knee and freed his partner's hand from the door. It remained frozen in a clawlike shape. "Tanya! Watch him; I've got to go get help!"

"Forget it, Mike," said Muntzy, his voice clogged. "Go ahead—go get 'em. Go—"

"No!" yelled Michael angrily. "You've got to hang on for just a minute." He braced the older man's shoulders. "Muntzy! You hear me? You've got to hang on!"

Muntzy relaxed in his partner's grasp, exhaling a final time. Michael fought to deny his Vietnam experience, which had taught him how to recognize that subtle diminishing of the body that is an irrefutable sign of death.

Onlookers began to edge warily toward them from the direction of the hotel and casino.

Michael looked up at Tanya. The blood had drained from his face and his hands were trembling. The terrible moment held, then burst. Michael rose and ran around to the driver's side. "Stay here with him, Tanya." The police chaser engine beneath the hood exploded into growling life.

Tanya leaned beside the lifeless form of Muntzy, jerking the passenger door open. "Michael! You can't leave Charles! You were hired to protect—"

"These people are no longer interested in your boss, Tanya. They just got what they wanted, and while we're wasting time they're putting more real estate between us and them, so *let go of the door!*"

She had to step over Muntzy's slack corpse, but she made it into the empty seat. "What are you talking about? I'm coming with you."

The front end of the vehicle heaved up and Michael laid down twin tracks of smoking rubber on the tarmac of the hotel lot. The thrust of their takeoff slammed Tanya's door closed for her.

As they cleared the lot Michael's eyes locked onto the road. "I know where they're headed for the rendezvous," he said. Single-handedly he yanked his service Magnum from under the driver's seat and snapped out the cylinder, spot-checking the hollow-point loads. "I don't have time to give you the whole story, Tanya— but Acton's own chief of security is up to his Bahamian bank accounts in industrial espionage . . . and he's just decided to graduate to first-degree murder."

"*Fred Wilson* a spy?" she said, aghast. "I don't believe it."

"Do you believe that dead cop back there?" he snapped. "Muntzy was my partner. I was supposed to be covering him and I blew it. And you saw how it went down in the casino a moment ago. One of the last things he said was *tres piedras*—meaning the Tres Piedras pullover. It's about nine miles from here. It's a rest stop for truckers that was bypassed when they rerouted the freeway to Reno. That's where they'll make the pass of whatever Wilson stole from Acton's room safe."

"But Wilson was in the casino nearly the whole time. I kept looking up and seeing him watching Charles and me."

"He had a partner." Michael's jaw was set, his expression grim. "And I had a partner, a damn good partner who spent six months with me trying to nail that snake. And now he's—" He cut himself off. "It's just over that rise ahead. Hang on to your seat, Tanya." He floored the pedal and the sleek car's needle introduced itself to the eighty mark.

The Consolidated security car had made killer time with its flash-bar lights, and those lights now lent crimson illumination to the gathering of three autos at the abandoned Tres Piedras truck rest stop. They were the only vehicles there. Beyond them was the night and scrub of the desert buffer surrounding Reno. The stars glittered in competition with the neon of the city. To any curious highway drivers the scene would resemble a simple pullover of a speeder by the highway patrol. All cop cars looked alike.

Fred Wilson came abreast of a wedge-shaped white Fiat. Beyond it was another security car from Consolidated, marked *Special Security*. From this third car stepped another operative named Symes, who tossed Wilson a little salute. To the driver of the Fiat Wilson said, "Would you step out of the car, please, ma'am?"

"Very funny," said Lonnie, opening her door and swinging out her well-molded legs, modeling them for an instant before standing and smoothing her diaphanous gown down over her trim and sumptuous figure. That shut everyone up. Toward Wilson she extended a tiny plastic cartridge of 16-mm subminiature slide film. Wilson sighed with relief.

The group was spun by the noise of Michael's car vaulting over the hillock at a hundred per and momentarily blinded by the high-beam lights coming, seemingly, from out of the sky. The chase car crunched to earth with brakes locked, turning broadside as it landed, skidding and kicking up a suffocating smoke-screen of dust. Michael leapt from his side of the car with his Magnum aimed and cocked full back before any of the knot of conspirators could react. The barrel favored Wilson's solar plexus.

The assassin Gray's hand hesitated midway into his coat.

"Wilson!" shouted Michael. "You move and I'll make your insurance company *very* happy!" He motioned with his pistol. "Nobody moves. I want your gun first, Wilson. Take it out barrel first, between your thumb and forefinger, and *lay* it, don't drop it, on the ground." Wilson did as he was told. "Very good. Now kick it toward me. No abrupt fast moves."

Wilson, his free hands extended in a kind of shrug, said to his companions, "May I present Michael Long—er, *Lieutenant* Michael Long, Mr. Acton's personal watchdog. We seem to have made a slight error . . ."

"Tanya, get over here." Michael cocked his head toward Wilson's gun, in the dirt several yards from his feet. He noticed that a smear of Muntzy's blood from the door panel of the car had discolored her expensive evening dress. She moved around to the front of Michael's car while Michael addressed Wilson: "Errors are okay, Wilson—you'll just have to put up with a *slight* death penalty. Tanya, pick up his gun."

From behind him Tanya said, "That won't be necessary, Michael. I have one of my own."

Wilson was smiling now. Gray and Symes relaxed. From next to the Fiat Lonnie glared at him, her gown wafting about in the slight desert breeze. Gray laughed first.

Michael's gun wavered as the nape of his neck prickled. Glancing back, he saw a tiny silver automatic in Tanya's hand, directed at the back of his head. As he turned he saw her other hand come up and brace the pistol in a professional firing grip. Now his body turned, trying to cover all the potential threat areas at once.

"You're working with them?" It was not a question.

"Ahh, I've disappointed you," she cooed, the sweet smile on her face decaying into something contemptible.

"Tanya. Give me the gun. You know if you cooperate with me I can—"

"You can nothing." He was facing down her barrel now.

His hand was out, not having given up yet. He kept his voice rational and reasoned. "Give it to me—?"

She smiled and nodded. "I intend to."

She fired into his face at a distance of slightly less than a yard and a half.

Michael catapulted backward with the impact, his gun flying away harmlessly. All he saw was the orange fire and bright red spray of the bullet plowing into his face. Then a firebrand of agony turned all his sensations into pain, plunged his perceptions into darkness. The conspirators were still laughing.

He began to slide down into death, resisting but helpless. He was theirs for the picking if they craved a bit of target practice. He was practically blind.

The laughing stopped and was replaced by the sound of steel-belted radials screeching away into the night. Nothing was left but the sound of his own idling engine. He knew his left hand was twitching uncontrollably but did not fight to stop it. It was all he could feel, spread-eagled there in the dirt.

Then he lost even that.

2

A searchlight split the night sky, sweeping over the dead terrain outside Reno in smooth arcs.

The twin turbine jet helicopter disrupted the still of the desert with its insect buzzing, and from an observation bubble in the fuselage of the machine, a dour, eroded face followed the track of the light.

The interior of the whirlybird was damped in the utter silence of expensive soundproofing baffles. The elderly man seated in the observation couch spoke into a throat mike, addressing the pilot: "Center on those headlights below and hover until I tell you to set down."

The helicopter swung through the air and went into a hover pattern over Michael Long's still-idling automobile. Splayed motionless, gruesomely spotlit by his own headlights, Michael lay in a widening mud puddle of his own blood. His face was a raw mask of obliterated tissue not even recognizably human.

"Oh my god," said the elderly man. "We're too late. Set it down, Mr. Harrison, and be quick. Alert the medical team and put them on emergency standby in case that boy's still among the living! And get me Miles on the double!"

He waited a moment for the patch to clear, then said, "Doctor, drink yourself some coffee and fire up the surgery theater. You're going to be working all night tonight. That's all. Patch me through to Devon."

After another beat he continued. "Devon, we've found our man but I'm afraid our friends, the corporate bandits, may have rendered him less than practical for our uses. I've appealed to Miles's good nature to persuade fate otherwise. On the off chance that the incompetent old quack succeeds, you must be prepared to mobilize the workshop immediately. I'll want the produce delivered in one week, no less, and no protests. Do you understand? And there's one other thing: we have the car. Mr. Sherman will be delivering it into your hands shortly."

A work crew leapt from the loading bay of the chopper before it even touched down, and worked with the speed and coordination of a crack firefight team.

Impatiently, Wilton Knight, monitoring all this action from his special bubble, chided the pilot: "Mr. Harrison, our subject is aboard; why haven't we taken off yet? Perhaps you'd prefer going back to a job covering freeway traffic jams?''

The helicopter tipped upward into the sky and made time south. From the bubble, Knight saw the crew member named Sherman pull Michael's car back onto the freeway and head back toward Reno, its lights dwindling to pinpoints on the road far below. In sixty seconds there was nothing left at Tres Piedras but a patch of blood slowly drying on the sand.

The medical research wing of Wilton Knight's sprawling two-hundred-acre estate had been constructed and staffed in early 1970. It was the habit of Knight Industries to plow profits back into research; this rule applied to all branches of the conglomerate—fiscal, legal, charitable—but most specifically to the research and development arms. Wilton Knight subscribed to the principle of self-interest in a big way, reasoning that if he could not cement his position as a corporate force with which to be reckoned, he would never gain the freedom to help people less fortunate. To that end, he stressed the importance of medical research and the refinement of surgical techniques . . . because he was old, and had fought many personal wars, and as a result was locked inside a body that was to prove his undoing. He intended to prolong his usefulness as long as was feasible with the help of his hand-picked medical staff. To finance the crushing expenditures caused by scientific research, he made sure that Knight Industries rode the wave of microprocessor technology that swept over the world during the decade of the 1970s. Knight Industries was in the vanguard in the incredibly costly support of space technology in an age where NASA had been all but gutted and stuffed by the government. Wilton Knight had made a habit of making ethical postures into personal crusades, and damning all expenses. This approach had cost him millions. But other equally audacious financial gambits had refilled his coffers, and Knight Industries had never tumbled into bankruptcy. Yet.

Knight's movements were infinitely slow and painful. He ignored Dr. Miles's advice to use the wheelchair more often, preferring to locomote under his own power, if for no other reason than to provide a constant example for those who worked on his behalf. He did use his cane, however—an ironwood monstrosity with a solid silver head, with which his grandfather, Mathias Knight, had beaten two highwaymen to death in the summer of 1870, in a small British town in Dorset. He used the head of the cane now to bang on the double doors of the medical research wing's operating theater before entering.

In the middle of banks of computerized equipment and rolling tables of monitors and tools, he found Dr. Miles tending to Michael Long.

"Well?" Knight boomed, as he hobbled across the room.

Dr. Miles did not look up. Instead he dropped

a chunk of cotton soaked in antiseptic into the sterile disposal tube and reached behind him. His hand located a thin penlight, which he used to examine Michael's pupils. He gingerly used one prong of a hemostat to move Michael's eyelids because Michael's entire head was swathed in thick bandages, and anchored, immobile, by a stainless-steel brace. He was sheeted to the neck, and intravenous hoses hung from one arm, feeding saline and glucose and occasionally, more plasma. Vital-signs monitors beeped and clicked erratically, their soft mechanical noises the only other sounds in the huge, hi-tech room.

Wilton Knight moved to the bedside and looked. He did not have to repeat himself.

"I'll give you the same answer I've given you the past four days," said Dr. Miles. "This boy is probably the only human being on the planet in worse condition than you."

"You have all the bedside manner of a rattlesnake."

"Thanks. My deal with you was honesty, remember?" For the first time he looked at Knight directly.

"Is he going to die or not?"

Dr. Miles replaced the hemostat and light on the tray. "If he was, I wish he'd go now. He must be in incredible pain. We can alleviate that somewhat, of course, but it's safer not to drug him so we can get true reactions to our tests—which sounds cruel, I realize, but—"

"Nonsense!" Knight said. "It's a more efficient way of keeping him alive. You may be inept when it comes to reassuring patients, doctor, but you know what you're doing."

"He *should* have died instantly," Dr. Miles emphasized.

"Except for the metal plate in his forehead," Knight said, tapping his own brow. "You told me about that the first night. What else have you found out about it?"

"The bullet was fired dead-center into his forehead at almost point-blank range," said the doctor. "It was a small-caliber slug from an Italian automatic, luckily for him. A bullet from a bigger gun, like the Magnum he usually carried, would have spread his skull all over the hood of his car, metal plate or not. As it was, the smaller slug struck the plate and splattered, spreading apart like a dumdum shell. It had no place to go and lots of velocity, so it flew back the way it came and took his face with it." He touched the helmetlike mass of bandages gently. "See? Everybody ought to have a little wartime souvenir in their head."

"Wartime?" Knight's eyes followed each adjustment made by Dr. Miles's capable hands.

"Yes—definite indications of military surgery, from the scars on his scalp. I'd estimate half of it was meatball surgery— you know, fast and dirty, to save his life— and the plate was the finesse work. They saved his life in a hurry; they knew when his hair grew back in it would hide the scars from the rough stitching."

Michael groaned from inside the mask of

appliances. Through a tiny slit in the bandages both men could see his lips moving. Most of the sounds were guttural; from the throat and diaphragm, not the mouth.

"What's he saying? Can you tell?" Knight was immediately interested.

"Can't tell," said Miles. "At least he's not in a coma. Here—keep an eye on him for a second." The doctor hurried across the room for a moment.

Knight saw Michael's thickly bandaged hand try to rise from the bed, hesitantly, as through struggling to defeat gravity. It dropped back and was still. But the guttural mumbling continued, and Knight fancied he recognized its tone.

He bent to the mask. "That's it son," he whispered. "Get mad . . . and stay mad. Your anger will keep you alive, keep you going when you run out of everything else. Just like mine is keeping me alive. Use your anger!"

Dr. Miles returned with a syringe. "He's okay?"

"Fine, doctor. I'm no medical man but I think he'll live." Knight braced himself against the edge of the bed. "But I've got to sit down."

Miles pushed a chair over and Knight slumped into it. Knight spotted the hypodermic needle and said, "I thought you said no drugs."

"Not for him. This is for you. It's that time of day again." He looked at Michael again. "He's asleep. At last. Good."

Knight unbuttoned his shirt cuff to receive

the injection, muttering under his breath. At least these shots were more dignified than the ones Miles insisted on injecting elsewhere. His withered hand stiffened on the silver head of his grandfather's walking stick as the needle punctured his skin.

Wilton Knight was the last of the Knight line. Both his brothers were already dead. Geoff, the eldest, had been childless, and died during the Normandy invasion while Wilt was working for OSS in Europe. The other had fathered two daughters and died in the crash of a commercial flight from New York to Denver in 1957. Drake Knight's daughters had both married into other names. The Knight line would die with Wilton.

And yet he had called the boy on the table "son."

Devon Miles moved quickly through the silent, vaulted hallway inside the Knight mansion. His lean, almost gaunt features were those of a bespectacled scientific benefactor, a chemist of white magic attired in a crisp business suit. He had an eternal air of vague distraction coupled with intense curiosity and a fatherly kind of benevolence. At the moment there was one other thing—a barely contained excitement.

He rounded a corner and came to a private room whose door was cracked open. Inside, Wilton Knight and Dr. Miles hovered over a hospital bed. None of this mattered to Devon, who spoke upon entering to Knight.

"I have good news for you! The Knight 2000 will be completely ready by—"

"Shhh!" Knight did not acknowledge Devon's entry, but silenced the offending interruption.

Mildly miffed, Devon froze in place, running his hand through his wavy gray hair. He pursed his lips, furrowed his brow and, when he saw that none of this mattered to the men working at the bedside, began muttering. "I work my people around the clock and suddenly you aren't interested. . . ."

Now he saw that Dr. Miles was peeling bandages, a layer at a time, from the head of the injured undercover policeman Knight had brought in many nights back. Curiosity overwhelmed his irritation, and he moved closer in order to see everything.

Miles lifted away the last strip of gauze and the three men stood around the bed, saying nothing.

With a nervous glance to the side, Michael Long said, "Is it that bad?"

Dr. Miles smiled. "On the contrary, young man, it's an excellent reconstruction job, if I do say so myself. The methods Knight Industries has perfected for using plastics have far surpassed—"

"Be quiet, Miles, and get the man a mirror!" Knight said sternly.

Miles handed a bureau hand mirror to Michael, who snatched it away and examined his new face.

Gone was the cast of features that had given him a kind of boyish charm, and substituted was a more rugged physiognomy. Now there was a jutting chin, sculpted cheekbones that made the eyes more intense and a classically Greek nose. The whole countenance would have seemed humorless and cold if not for the sensuously full lips.

Michael moved to touch his face and was impeded by the bandages covering his fingertips. "Why are my hands bandaged?" he said, and promptly forgot his question, setting about poking and rubbing his new face despite fat wads of gauze. "It isn't *me*," he said, his voice very small.

"Don't poke it too much, or you might push the nose off center," said Dr. Miles, and Michael jerked his hand quickly away before realizing it was a joke.

"Perfection," said Knight from the foot of the bed. "You now have a second chance to live . . . unless, of course, you'd prefer to walk the earth with a face that could get you killed all over again." He stifled the question he knew Michael was about to ask. "Take my word for it. You'll be much safer with this face. And it *is* rather handsome . . . if I may be permitted the observation."

Devon narrowed his eyes at Michael, taking a second to judge before speaking. "It's *you*," he said to Knight. "It *is* you." To counter Knight's laser-beam gaze he quickly added, "Well, the Wilton Knight of forty or so years ago, to be sure, but the resemblance is uncanny." Then he conceded, uncomfortably. "I'm sure it's just my imagination."

Dr. Miles might have told Devon that he had worked from photographs in the rebuilding of Michael's face, but he wisely kept silent. And the photos, of a younger Wilton Knight in his OSS days, were safely back in their dusty file folders.

"Stick to your field, Devon," admonished Knight. "When will I see it?"

"I tried to tell you. It'll be ready within the week."

"Excellent, excellent," he said, not taking his sight from Michael. "I pray your schedule will leave me enough time."

No one, not even Michael, asked what *that* meant.

Knight propped his elbows on the eroded stone balustrade of the mansion's second-story terrace and peered through a pair of highpowered Cox binoculars, his heirloom cane hooked over one forearm. In the distance Michael Long jogged around the perimeter of what was once the estate's polo grounds but was now merely an expanse of lush green lawn. He was clad in blue shorts and tennis shoes, and Knight kept tabs on his progress from his seat on the terrace.

"I envy him the motion," Knight said to Devon.

"How much have you told him?"

Knight pondered for a moment before responding. "I told him he no longer has anyone to fear, and that in the eyes of the law, the entity known as 'Michael Long' is legally dead."

"But, Mr. Knight," Devon said uncomfortably. "Stealing a corpse from the medical school for the investigators to find at Tres Piedras wasn't exactly playing by the rules. It smacks of grave robbery. Of what Burke and Hare did for the infamous Dr. Knox . . . only in reverse."

May I remind you that I make my own rules, Devon, as does the government. They fake deaths and erase identites all the time; they construct people who never existed and document them back to the fifth generation— and never for so noble a cause as ours. Our adversaries, I am at pains to point out, don't *exactly play by the rules* either. Not by the marquis of queensberry's rules, not by Hoyle . . . nothing so honorable." He watched Michael make another circuit of the field.

"All right, fine—but why are you doing it in just this one case, then?"

"I think you know why, Devon." He smiled, but it was edged with impatience, because he knew Devon had already guessed and was inquiring anyway. That was a scientist for you—empirical and infinitely redundant. "I want to leave something behind when I go. Something worthwhile, not just a corporate history and numbers in a bank account—a legacy of compound interest and dividends to put roses on my grave." He rubbed his eyes wearily, and set the binoculars down. "Now. About the Knight 2000—is it ready?"

"Soon. I've got my crews on double shifts."

"Go to around the clock, effective immediately. We must hurry, Devon."

Devon sobered, and asked with honest concern, "Has the doctor told you—?"

"Don't worry about what the good doctor did or did not tell me. Just get those crews of yours hopping. Let me worry about the doctors . . . and about Mr. Michael Long."

Michael was puffing laboriously now, trying to burn off a last hundred yards in scant seconds. When he turned off the field, it was to run up the wide stone steps to the terrace. He saw Devon's lanky form close the french doors and recede inside the mansion.

Knight watched the younger man's chest expand and contract, throwing the lean, sinewy build into hard relief. Sweat dripped from Michael's chin. Standing still after all the exertion was clearly a mild shock.

"Aren't you pushing a bit too hard, Michael?" said Knight, his tone unmistakably paternal.

"You can never get back into shape fast enough." He snatched up a towel from the circular café table and daubed at himself. "I've got an outstanding debt of the old Michael Long's to pay off."

With a sidelong glance of irritation, Knight said, "Is revenge all you can think about?" He sipped a tepid cup of tea, one of the two cups per day he was still permitted by Dr. Miles's strict diagnosis.

"Trails get cold fast in the desert," Michael said simply. "Or don't you know what hap-

pened to Muntzy? You seem to know everything else about me already." He dragged up
a lawn chair and sat down. From a pitcher on
the table he helped himself to some tea, without ice.

"You were a good cop, too," said Knight.
"Would that good cop just go plunging headlong into such a vendetta as you're thinking
of now without really thinking in the first
place? You're better than that, surely."

Michael sensed he was being challenged.
"Was I?" He said with some bitterness. "I
blew it. Six months of work, stakeouts, deep
cover, investigations, and I blew it all in less
time than it takes to run around your private
rugby field over there."

Knight steepled his fingers in thought.
"What if I could offer you another shot? You
see, I want Tanya Walker and her little circus
of thieves, too. You may have noticed that
Charles Acton and I are in related industries,
both heavily dependent on microchip technology, and equally vulnerable to moral ter-
mites like our dear, beautiful, lethal Tanya.
But she and her kind are just the tip of an
iceberg of corruption and espionage-for-profit.
If you and I were to work in concert with
each other, Michael, and—"

"Mr. Knight," Michael said, standing. "My
last partner is dead. Nothing personal, but
from now on I work alone. I can't take the
responsibility for anyone's life but my own,
now. There's been too much death. If you've

read my records, you should be able to understand that."

It was a melodramatic exit, but he jogged down the steps without allowing Knight to say anything further. He ran, trying to shove his tiring body beyond its limit of endurance. The names and faces of the past welled up from the dead files of his memory as he ran, trying— unsuccessfully—to blot them out.

First, his father had succumbed leukemia when Michael was only seven years old. His mother, once an attractive woman, had been killed an inch at a time by her obsessive pursuit of the blue-collar dream. Overwork murdered her. Two weeks after her funeral, Michael had joined the Green Berets, with the first layers of emotional callus that would make him such a good undercover man already hardening him at age twenty.

Michael strained to go faster, legs pumping, exhaling his psychic decay as he ran.

Then came the memories of Vietnam, and the weeks of living crowded against death's shoulder. As bad as his intelligence work had gotten during the first two years overseas— eight times he had been required to kill interlopers with his bare hands, and one of those had been a diminutive, pretty double agent from the An Loc region—it was nothing compared to the POW camp that had been his home and personal hell for the third year.

Almost by accident, Michael Long had found himself boxed in in the midst of a Viet Cong smash-and-grab raid, unconscious by a bullet splinter. When he awoke, the raiders were gone, and he found himself in the custody of the North Vietnamese. Battle was neat and well defined compared to the tiger cages, tortures and interrogations that ensued. Michael found himself losing his time sense; his perception of pain became almost a pleasurable thing since he could use it to define time. Pain—as Wilton Knight had reminded him in the operating theater—proved you were alive, at least. Michael spent three agonizing months planning the logistics of his escape from the POW corral. When he implemented his plan—at the point when further questions and the subtle tortures of which the Viet Cong were capable would have made him irreclaimably insane—it went off with but one hitch. His depleted physical condition made overpowering a Cong sentry more difficult than he was prepared for, and he sustained a skull fracture in the struggle, complicating the damage already done by the stray bullet that had hit him during his capture. For a day and a half he tried to evade capture while fighting disorienting waves of reality distortion and vertigo. He survived by willpower, or sheer metabolic stubbornness, and when he collapsed into the arms of a grubby American sergeant spearheading a patrol in the To Noc Wah basin, he was on the cliff edge of death.

Forty-eight hours later he awoke inside the tented confines of an army surgical unit, with a metal plate in his skull and a tromping dinosaur of a headache.

Back in the States, he returned to his birth-
place in Reno and linked up with the police
force in 1972. He was a rookie cop during the
rash of bomb threats designed to extort money
from casinos that plagued Nevada in the early
and mid-1970s. Frequently Michael found himself up against syndicate slugs and cockroaches
who controlled key gambling establishments.
The only thing that was not new was the
quotient of death he had to deal with on a
daily basis.

His first partner, a jocular German named
Hart Kinder, was killed in the parking lot of a
topless joint in west Reno, during a gang
shootout that lasted forty-five minutes and
cost seven lives. In 1978, during the pickup of
an illegal arms dealer who had attended a
gun show held at one of the casino hotel
showrooms, another partner, one Bryan Mac-
Dermott, stopped a gas-tipped armor-piercing
slug with his forehead. MacDermott had been
a family man, and the burden of death had
fallen to Michael.

Then came 1982, and the detective's shield,
and the partnership with Ralph "Muntzy"
Muntz—another cop recently deprived of a
partner. Michael and Muntzy were the force's
odd couple, the swashbucklers of the squad.
They quickly racked up an impressive roster
of stings and arrests that led to the Consolidated Chemical assignment. Their key infor-
mant had been Tanya Walker . . . who had
been such an efficient turncoat that both Michael and Muntzy got eclipsed.

Tanya Walker. So Knight had a beef against her, too, thought Michael, finally changing course and making for the wing of the mansion where his bed was. It was clear that Knight intended to extract some sort of favor from him in return for saving his life. Michael was appreciative, and would do almost anything the old man wanted . . . but not until after he took Tanya down.

He glanced back toward the terrace. Wilton Knight was gone.

From the air, the Knight estate's single largest structure was an enormous shell of corrugated steel that could have easily done service as a zeppelin hangar. Surrounded by a concrete lip and connected on the north to the estate's private airstrip, the eastern doors of this structure were fully seventy-five feet high. One half of the interior of the building was a vast, open testing space conveniently roofed against the elements. The other half was a multistoried honeycomb of laboratories, testing cubicles, controlled experimental environments, comfortably furnished think tanks and warehouse facilities. This was one of the comprehensive scientific research and development superstructures maintained by Knight Industries.

Within the cool, dark confines of 11-B, an electronics lab, Wilton Knight shifted his weight off his cane and rested against a workbench scattered with components. As in the medical section, there seemed to be monitors constantly beeping and clicking here even when there was not an experiment in progress. From an audio speaker flush against the tool peg-board came the strains of Bach's Prelude and Fugue No. 5 in D major, a light, airy piano piece.

Devon closed the lab door behind him. "It's ready," he said with obvious pride.

Knight nodded. "I know. So are we. We have our man. I'm sure of it."

"Wilton, you already know I've never been in total agreement with your intended applications of the FLAG project." When Devon grew serious, he always grew personal, and Knight took no umbrage at the familiar use of his first name. After the smoke cleared, he and Devon were essentially close friends despite their different approaches. "But even if I were," Devon continued, "I'd question the choice of Michael Long. First of all, he's too young—"

"He'll need to be young, Devon. Or are you just a little bit jealous?"

"*And* inexperienced." Devon did not let Knight's gibe distract him.

"He worked virtually alone in Vietnam for three years in counterintelligence, under deep cover."

"He was captured," countered Devon.

"He survived capture, and he escaped. A lot of his captors did *not* survive."

"You could say the same thing for a lot of his partners. I'll agree with you that he works well on his own. That's what disturbs me

most about this particular choice—what you
have in mind, Wilton, what *we* hope to accomplish, demands teamwork. Can we afford
a random, unstable element like Michael Long?
A maverick?"

"He's going to be on his own in the field
most of the time, Devon. Can we *not* afford
someone who is a survivor, a resourceful agent
who can think on his feet?"

Devon sighed. "Of course, at first. But
eventually, in the long run, when we prove—"

"When *we* prove, Devon," said Knight.
"That's the key. Our boy is going to be our
living proof, our walking vindication, our
living, breathing demonstration that each of
us as *individuals* can make a difference in the
world. People really believe they don't matter
anymore. Our society is crippled by cog-in-
the-wheel thinking. Our country's population
has thrown up its arms in disgust and sub-
mitted, accepting imposed roles as consumers,
convinced their opinions are so much chaff in
a hurricane because their individual votes
are a joke. Conformity and the lowest com-
mon denominator are emphasized. People are
made to actually believe that they don't know
what's good for them, that they don't have a
dendrite of intelligence in their heads, and
along comes an assault force of psychologists
and psychiatrists to let them know that they
aren't responsible for their own actions. Al-
coholism, obesity, even *anger* have become
diseases—topped off by that great disease of
the twentieth century, stress . . . which didn't

exist before the analysts invented it. It all boils down to diminishing the individual and abrogating personal responsibility. All of our greatest visionaries have been individualists willing to be responsible human beings. Usually they're crushed by the status quo. But Devon, where would *I* be today if I had been a conformist, a herd member, instead of the headstrong pain in the behind you know me to be? Isn't it time for one man, one visionary, to help resuscitate the concept of will?"

Devon worked his hands together. "Why do I always attempt to challenge your instincts with logic? I always lose. . . ."

"Because you're a first-rate scientist. But from your so-called 'loss,' we both win. Believe me, Devon—Michael Long is our man. You'll have to concede to a feeling."

"Then I'll ask you—how do you want to play it?"

Knight smiled. "Our boy has taken to wandering the grounds at night. No doubt in some kind of guilt-ridden reverie, feeding off his hatred for Tanya Walker and her cohorts. He'll find his way to the testing bay, never fear."

Crickets chattered.

Michael had wakened in a sweat from a nightmare in which Tanya's face, the split instant before the gunshot, floated like a specter of death—lovely, yet fatal. Then the orange fire washed everything away.

He walked the grounds without destination, sucking cool draughts of night air. Tracing his jogging track was not sufficiently distracting, and so he wandered in the direction of the imposing, hangarlike structure on the northwest lip of the grounds, near the airfield where the helicopter had airlifted him in. Doubtlessly it was used for one of Knight Industries' manufacturing pursuits.

As he drew closer he saw that the seventy-five-foot doors were split by a band of black two feet in width. He suppressed a manic grin. Hell of a place to leave unlocked and unguarded, he thought.

It was utterly dark inside. He eased between the parted doors.

A private Lear jet was parked just inside, and Michael ducked under a wingtip. His footsteps began to echo in the vast, interior space. It was like being in the belly of an impossibly huge oil tanker, the sheer space dwarfing even the plane and making it seem toylike.

He heard a grumbling noise. It sounded like a pump or engine of some kind, overlaid with a very faint turbine whine. He lost the sound of his footsteps amid the new and growing noise. Some kind of maintenance machinery, he thought, maybe an air purifier. He extended his arms in the dark like antennae, seeking the direction of the idling noise, which surrounded him in the poor acoustics of the hangar.

Michael turned as a glowing red eye sought him in the dark. Tiny in the distance, a horizontal bar of faceted crimson light tracked

back and forth like the LEDs on a police-band
radio.

He began to walk toward the oscillating
red light, and the engine noise grew louder as
he approached.

Suddenly two blazing, fog-cutting lamps
popped up on either side of the tracking red
light, nailing Michael between them. Automobile high beams.

The echoing engine noise revved mightily,
and before Michael could react, the vehicle
that had been waiting for him peeled out on
the traction surface of the hangar floor and
bore down on him with an amazing jolt of
acceleration. The high beams grew huge. He
was trapped in the open, he could see by the
light, with no place to run where the car
could not overtake and crush him.

It was a trap, he thought frantically, running anyway. A trap, and you walked right
into it. Again.

He heard the car gaining on him.

He looked over his shoulder and the headlights blinded him. There was no place left to
run.

3

Michael waited until the heat of the headlights warmed his backside before he dived
abruptly sideways, tucked and rolling on the
concrete floor to the right of the machine. He
saw it slide into a power turn in the space he
had just left. Tires whining on the floor, the
juggernauting black vehicle broadsided around
as Michael regained his balance, skidding to
a stop with the driver's side door several inches
away from his face.

It was his own car, the sleek black street
machine.

As he pushed to his feet a hundred maintenance floods kicked on all around the inside
of the hangar, with the car theatrically pinned
by a spray of hot yellow light. Its finish glittered blackly like the carapace of some ebony
animal, smooth and flawless.

Wilton Knight's voice boomed cavernously

inside the hangar: "Enough, Devon. You've had your little bit of fun with our guest."

Michael did a double take, seeing that Devon was installed in the pilot seat of the car.

Wilton Knight was limping toward them from the underside of the parked Lear jet.

Devon buzzed the window down on the driver's side. To Michael he said, "It's not polite to sneak about restricted areas uninvited, you know."

"Be gracious, Devon," said Knight, catching up with them. "I think an explanation is well overdue."

Fear and adrenaline had shifted into anger for Michael. "You're bloody damned right it is! What the hell is all this? You creep around this joint in the dark, in the middle of the night—"

"Look who's talking," Devon said wryly.

"Quiet, both of you," interposed Knight. "We have business to get down to. I'm running low on time. And Michael is now healthy enough to carry on.".

In the center of the broad, open area, the three men formed a triad of opposition. Michael thought, here it comes. Knight's big punch line for me; the price he wants to extract for saving my hide. "Carry on what?" he said immediately, and too loudly. "Look—I never agreed to be part of you plans and have no idea what it is you're doing here. All I have to carry on with is a score to settle, and a life to get back to living!"

Devon shook his head like an exasperated

schoolteacher. "Now you're not being very gracious. Or grateful."

Michael looked back to Wilton Knight. "The guys you're after are too big! Can't you understand that! They're the kind of people who can operate above the law. Nobody can even touch them!"

"I don't agree with you," Knight said softly.

"You're entitled to your opinion." Michael sneered. "But as for me, I'm pulling out of here *tonight*. My car is ready, I'm okay, and I'm leaving. . . ." A look of hesitancy fleetingly crossed his face. "Devon, get out of my car. I mean it."

Devon started to protest but Knight cut in: "Prepare the car for Michael, Devon. There's a great deal he'll need to know about it before it is safe for him to drive, if he is just going to take off as he insists." He turned away, not even seeing Michael. "Now you'll excuse me. I need to get to bed. I'm not feeling very well." Knight made his way out of the hangar, limping along with the help of his silver-headed cane.

Devon kicked the car door open and stood face-to-face with Michael. For a moment Michael thought the beneficent scientist was going to punch him in the nose. Instead he looked after Wilton Knight. "You've just hurt a dying man," he said with a fatal calm that stung Michael deeply.

"Hey, Devon, listen—I like that old man. I really do. But it's time to get on with my life and—"

"Yes, let's discuss your all-important life!" Devon said with a grimace. "You haven't let the facts penetrate your young, thick, upstart head. Perhaps it's the metal plate that keeps you from receiving the truth. You wouldn't have a life if it were not for Wilton Knight's intervention! And even if you had survived, disfigured permanently or not, there would still be people hunting for you, anxious to finish you off." He made a little snort of disgust.

Michael rubbed his face, feeling foolish. Devon was right, and he was being worse than an ingrate. "Okay, okay," he said, cooling off. "But maybe you don't understand how important it is for me to nail Tanya and Fred Wilson and that bunch."

"I understand too well. What you don't see is that we can accomplish your aims—and ours—as a team, which is what Wilton Knight wants."

"I'm legally dead, Devon. It's the deepest cover there is. I don't even know the face I'm wearing." To distract himself from the topic, he pointed to the car. "Just what the devil is so special about my car now, other than you using it to scare the crap out of me?" He pointed again. "And why does it all of a sudden have a death ray in the hood . . . or whatever that red light is?"

"Any resemblance between your old car and its reincarnation—if you'll pardon the pun—is purely superficial."

Michael bent to examine the light bank in the hood. "What are you talking about? This is *my car*. I left it in the desert, at Tres Piedras. What's there to know? It's black. It has four wheels. The gearshift knob jiggles if I go above seventy-five. It's got a death ray in the hood."

"No. It may *look* like your car. But in actuality this vehicle is probably the most expensive car in the world." He folded his hands, smugly.

"What are you talking about?" Michael ran his hand along the smooth contour of the right fender. "Hey—what is this, new paint?" He bent close, looking to Devon for explanation. "Feels like . . . I don't know, baby skin. Not a ripple in it. Nice work." He knocked softly on it. "Very pretty. A dentist could use this finish as a mirror for drilling. . . ."

"It's not paint," said Devon. "It's a finish bonded into the molecular structure of the car body itself, a—"

"You mean the metal?"

"Not metal," Devon affirmed. "Not fiberglass either. A new substance altogether. An alloy only space technology could produce." From the floor of the car Devon withdrew a large ball-peen hammer. "Here. Hit it."

Michael looked at the hammer, a fourteen-inch shaft of wood terminating in several pounds of drop-forged steel. *"Hit* my car with this?"

"Strike the finish as hard as you can."

"No way! I like it the way it is!"

Devon allowed himself a tolerant little smile, as though he were explaining an infinitely simple process to a dull student. He took the hammer from Michael and raised it over his head, putting his shoulder into the blow.

"Wait!" Michael yelled.

With a muted *thump*, the rounded end of the hammer hit the area where Michael's hand had caressed the finish a moment before. It bounced off the surface with such rebound force that it flew free of Devon's grasp and spun, clattering, to the floor between the two men.

The point of impact was unmarked, pristine, flawless.

Michael's voice was tiny with awe. "How did you do that?"

"Don't stand there gawking. Get in."

Michael moved to the open driver's door, and for the first time saw the modified panels curving out of the dashboard. The steering wheel had been replaced by a fat-handled device similar to a jet's two-handed joystick. Readout screens and telltales blinked and glittered. Where the dials had been was now a black glassine field alive with varicolored neon digits and constantly fluctuating bar gauges. To the lower left and right of the wheel were unobtrusive control boxes with lighted, heat-sensitive pushbuttons. Michael saw another such unit on the transmission hump next to the gearshift lever. Twenty lighted buttons there, plus a pair of larger toggles. On the ceiling near the mirror mount was another group of digitized switches. On the curvature where the modified steering column sloped up to blend with the spacy flow of the dash was a screen that swam with red color, flanked by function lights. Below that were more function bars, each a different color. He squinted and read: AUTO CRUISE. NORMAL CRUISE. PURSUIT. To the right of the wheel he also saw a pair of TV Monitor screens mounted side by side. Below them was a blinking red toggle in the shape of a stop sign. A panic button, maybe?

Carefully, Michael fit himself into the brown plush of the driver's bucket.

Devon leaned in. "Welcome aboard the Knight 2000."

"Uh . . . thanks," he said, eyes a bit glassy. "I'll bet you're going to tell me what all this stuff is for, right? This looks like the Batmobile."

"This is a unique car, Michael. One of a kind. It is faster, safer and stronger than any automobile in the world." With a confident air of superiority that in any lesser man would have signaled gloating, Devon rattled off more facts: "It is hydrogen-fueled and totally fuel-efficient. The microprocessors that control its functions make it impossible for the vehicle to be involved in any sort of mishap or collision . . . unless specifically ordered to by its pilot."

Michael looked doubtfully at Devon. "You mean it flies, too?"

"Of course not. This car *thinks*."

"You mean like those Japanese imports that tell you to buckle your seat belt, or take out the garbage, or empty the ashtrays?"

Devon cleared his throat, reaching in and punching several buttons. The engine fired up instantaneously, filling the hangar with the hissing energy noise Michael had noticed earlier. "I suppose we must begin at the beginning. Now, in order to motivate forward . . ."

"Devon, I'm not a moron. I mean, there are a few of the more rudimentary controls I recognize, such as the accelerator. I *do* know how to drive, you know. Special Nevada police offensive-driving training. Top of my class." Impatiently, he reached around Devon's pointing finger and depressed a yellow rectangular button. It made a touch-tone noise when he pressed it, expecting the car to drop electronically into first gear.

The sleek black auto jumped forward like a horizontally aimed missile, spinning Devon and slamming the pilot door shut with the force of takeoff.

Michael's hands jumped to the wheel and he saw tall red digits accumulating on the left panel with the speed of a time clock at the Olympics: 75, 85, 99, 105 . . .

The hangar doors stood open with only two feet of space between them. There was not time to do anything except stomp on the brakes and brace for the crash. Michael's eyes squeezed shut involuntarily.

The speeding car blew through the metal warehouse doors like a brick through a plate-glass window, knocking thousands of bits of fragmented steel everywhere. Michael saw the doors disintegrate around him as he punched through. The car nosed down hard as it went from a fast 110 mph to zero in an instant. It sat outside idling, waiting for another task.

Michael couldn't get out of the car fast enough.

Devon peeked out through the demolished double doors. "I really would have preferred you to let me open the doors first. However . . ."

Michael turned, eyes wide. "There's not a scratch on this thing. That door was made out of metal!"

"Mm. Reinforced industrial steel. I *did* just tell you about the alloy. I thought my implication was clear: this car is virtually indestructible."

"Very nice," said Michael, still shaken. "You also said it couldn't have a collision, and it just did."

"That's because you have to turn the system on for it to be operable. I was coming to that when you interceded."

"Oh."

Devon walked around him, reached inside and pressed a few more buttons. It sounded like he was punching in a long-distance phone number.

Michael eyed the car warily. "Now you say I can't hit anything?"

Devon bowed. "Trust me."

"I'll never trust anybody again!" But he climbed back into the aerodynamic black shape.

Devon ducked into the passenger seat next

to him and buckled his shoulder strap, motioning for Michael to do likewise.

He sat flexing his hands before the controls. "I'm warning you, Devon. I'm going to put this thing to the test. Now. What do I do first?"

"You step on the accelerator. You said you knew what one looked like." Devon sat, eyes front, completely deadpan.

"Right." Michael gripped the wheel and floored the pedal, aiming the car for the service road that led to the main gate of the Knight estate. A uniformed security guard rushed to push the gate back before the streaking car caught up with him and then tipped his cap to Devon as the auto blasted past, kicking up a tail wind.

Devon proudly explained other facets of the car as they found their way to the highway, deserted of traffic in the wee hours except for the ever-present truckers making their long, cross-country hauls.

"You'll notice that the dash panels fit the contour of the human arm—*your* arm, to be exact, Michael. The cockpit is fitted out to your dimensions to decrease fatigue. The function buttons on the transmission hump are arranged in what we call a 'typewriter sequence,' which simply means that after your indoctrination your hands will be able to land on the correct switches without you looking to check. You'll know the location of each specific function by feel."

They were gaining fast on a lumbering semitractor rig in the right lane.

"I can't buy this," said Michael uncomfortably. "A scientist is making me play chicken with a ten-ton semi."

"Take your hands off the wheel," said Devon calmly. "And—what is the expression?—put the pedal to the metal!" They were already doing ninety.

"You mean just crash into his tailgate?"

The trucker saw them hugging his tail and gave them a warning blast on his air horn, thinking the driver of the bulletlike black racer had passed out at the wheel.

"You won't crash into anything. Do it."

Michael released the wheel and fatalistically watched the red neon digits pile up past one hundred.

The truck, which was moving on an upgrade in low gear, was unable to pull over, get out of the path of the maniac in the black car or speed up. Its driver braced for the thump of the auto hitting its tailgate.

The black car sliced around the semi at the last possible second before impact, dodging out, the digital speedometer recording a burst of acceleration that jumped Devon and Michael to 130 as the truck blurred past to the right and shrank away rapidly in the mirrors. Then the car zipped back into the right-hand lane and burned along at a steady 100 mph. Michael's hands were still off the wheel.

His mouth was working but nothing was coming out.

"Marvelous, isn't it?" said Devon, utterly composed.

"It just . . . steered itself around the truck!"

"You're belaboring the obvious, Michael. How do you like it?"

"I hate it." That surprised Devon. They turned to face each other, Michael suddenly grabbing the wheel, then remembering the car was on some incomprehensible form of automatic pilot. Sheepishly, he released the wheel. He did not know what to do with his hands.

Devon was waiting for an explanation while the countryside flew past outside.

"I like to make my own decisions. Driving is as much a matter of instinct as skill," Michael said finally.

"The microprocessor deduced that you were making a decision—that is, accelerating and removing your hands from the wheel—that was counter to your best interests. It had two options: slow the car down, or maneuver around the obstacle."

"So why didn't it slow down? That would have been much safer. What if there was another truck in the oncoming lane? We were too close to see around the first one, and we were going too fast to divert."

"Well, I . . ." Devon looked pained. "Ah—"

"Come on, come on," chided Michael, happy for the advantage. "I think I just found a flaw in your baby, your perfect machine. Yes?"

"It's not that. It isn't a flaw."

Michael tracked over the various panels

again. There were more indicators in this rig
than in the Space Shuttle.

"The car was showing off for you," Devon
said.

"What!" He grabbed the wheel and added,
"How do I slow this thing down!"

Devon depressed a button and the AUTO
CRUISE lightbar in front of Michael went dark.
Two red pinpoint telltales shifted position,
and when Michael stepped on the brake the
car dragged heavily with deceleration. The
red neon numerals dropped off to a safe, legal
fifty-five.

"You mean this thing can just decide to
take off whenever it *wants* to? Cruise off on
its own to get gas or a wash and wax? That'd
be terrific if you just happened to be under
the hood or chassis when it got restless."

"Oh, it wouldn't do anything to harm you, I
assure you," Devon said. "In fact, its primary
function is to preserve human life. Specifically,
your life. We have taken one of Asimov's fic-
tional Laws of Robotics and made it flesh . . .
so to speak."

"You mean it protects anyone driving?"

Devon fixed his eyes on the road. "No. I
mean *you*. The vehicle is personalized in more
ways than just a good fit for your body. It's
keyed, geared and modified precisely for you.
Michael Arthur Long." He expelled a heavy
breath. He had serious reservations. "Soon to
become Michael Knight."

"What—?"

A tiny peeping noise sounded in the car,

and when Devon lifted his arm in response, Michael saw a miniscule diode on his wrist-watch blinking an urgent red.

"We must get back to the mansion immediately," Devon said. *"Now*, Michael. Wilton Knight is in trouble."

The two men hit the door to the east wing at a dead run. The first person they saw was Dr. Miles, standing anxiously at the door to Wilton Knight's sleeping chamber.

"You two had better hurry," he said simply. Horribly.

Michael shouldered past him, first into the huge bedroom. Below a mantel of solid quarry marble from Italy, a fire of cedar logs burned vigorously, making the air in the room dense with warmth. The floor-to-ceiling draperies were drawn, and their rich burgundy velvet reflected the firelight softly. Wilton Knight lay in his canopied four-poster bed, his form barely impressing the coverlet and comforter, his head barely denting the pillows. His withered, clawlike hands were folded on his chest. He looked like the deadest thing in the world.

As Devon moved past him Michael said, "God. We're too late."

Knight's eyes clicked open. "You mean almost too late. What's the matter—car not fast enough for you?"

Devon was visibly relieved. "Wilton, are you all right?"

"No."

Devon turned to summon Dr. Miles back

into the room as Michael moved to Knight's bedside.

"Listen, Mr. Knight . . . I don't know what to say. I do know that you've got to put that machine on the market. It could save thousands of lives . . . there's never been anything as sophisticated."

Knight's eyes rolled to meet Michael's. The old man was in obvious pain, and he spoke with infinite care, as though by choosing fewer words he could conserve what energy remained in him. "Put it on the market and have it taken away from me? Tied up in contracts, *stolen* and locked away by the auto manufacturers so it doesn't cut into their profits? Let the Tanya Walkers of the world purloin it the way my aircraft designs were purloined—and suppressed? My turbine drive? My nonpolluting fuels? No, Michael, I've given up that way. I have other plans for that car."

"Please, Wilton," urged Devon, seeing that Knight's anger was causing dangerous strain. "Let me explain."

"No. Michael, come closer. Please."

A stone fist closed inside of Michael, chilling him. He sensed imminent death in the air.

"Think about the opportunity I'm offering you," Knight pressed on. "You don't exist. You're legally dead. No one can trace your identity—or your source of funds and support." His voice had sunk away to a rasping whisper. "Even your fingerprints have been altered.

Dr. Miles calls the technique acid-whorl sculpting."

Involuntarily, Michael glanced at his fingertips. "The bandages on my hands when I woke up . . ." Anger boiled inside him again. "This *opportunity* was all a setup. I used to do set-ups for a living, only we called them stings." His fists closed.

"*You* set yourself up," said Knight, "when you still had faith in the idea that one man could make a difference. That's what sent you to war, what put you on the police force when you had already faced enough death and catastrophe to discourage lesser men. But this most recent 'sting,' the one that cost Mr. Muntz his life and almost cost you yours, has disillusioned you. I want you to get that spirit back before it's too late. I want it to become your obsession . . . as it has become my own."

Dr. Miles moved in unobtrusively to minister to Knight.

"You seem determined to make me in your own image," Michael said.

"Michael!" Devon's voice rose in embarrassment.

Something warred inside Michael, and suddenly he found an obstruction in his throat. "Mr. Knight, I . . ." He swallowed hard. All of a sudden he felt an impending sense of doom. "Look, you saved my life, and I don't want to appear ungrateful or cruel. But maybe I was supposed to die out there at Tres Piedras. Death is an accepted fact of my life. I've always accepted it. And I've been prepared to face it ever since I was a little seven-year-old kid. Don't make me so noble, because I'm not. I just didn't care if I got killed, and that made me appear daring and brave. And I'd like to be able to promise you that I could take on the world on your behalf someday ... but I can't. I used to have a real life, and some real friends, but now all I have is a nightmare—a bad dream where the barrel of that little gun that almost did me in is as big as the Bay Ridge Tunnel, and I wake up shaking at the point where it belches orange fire and the whole world blows apart."

"Don't deny that; I'm not asking you to," said Knight. "Embrace that moment of death. Remember it, and make it your baptism by fire. You were spared to lead a great fight."

Michael's voice was weak. "I'm not a leader."

"All right, an example, then. Don't turn away in fear. You can prove that one human being can make all the difference in the world. You're the revolutionary, the outcast, the visionary. You're the man who can make a difference ... if you'll accept my legacy."

"I can't stand here and baldly lie to you, Mr. Knight." Michael faltered. "I just don't know if—"

"*I* know. I'm sure." With great effort, alarming Dr. Miles, Knight reached out for Michael. His hand rose slowly off the bed and opened weakly.

Michael found his eyes filling up with tears against his will. Knight's extended hand hovered precariously in the air between them.

"If you refuse me," Knight said, "then my entire life has come to nothing. Dust and ashes."

Michael reached forward and clasped the old man's hand in both of his, surprising himself with the emotion.

Knight's eyes slid closed, as though he had just achieved release. "My adventure has ended," he said. "Yours has just begun." Then his final breath left him and his body relaxed. His hand became dead weight in Michael's.

At first what Michael felt inside himself was no different than the anguish he had experienced at Muntzy's death. But then he fixed on Wilton Knight's dead countenance. There was an expression there that he had never before seen on a dead person. Michael's senses informed him unerringly that the man was dead; that Dr. Miles's checking was superfluous. But there was something new to his experience—a look of utter peace on Wilton Knight's face. He watched it and tried to fathom its meaning.

After a long while, after Devon and Dr. Miles had left him alone in the room, Michael placed Wilton Knight's hand gently back on his chest.

4

The funeral was no different than the dozens of others Michael had attended in his lifetime. For Wilton Knight's obsequies the trappings were as lush as the phony green hue of the cemetery lawn, but the grass, the tons of flowers in memorial wreaths, and the dead black high fashion of the congregation of mourners were all just window dressings— props seeing one more dead man along on what the papers would call his "final voyage." it was always called something other than plain death.

The newspaper hounds were present, of course, along with other media. Michael wheeled away from the graveside and walked with swift strides to one of the black limousines parked along a curving scenic drive. As he passed a newsman standing before a video team, disrupting the perfection of their shot, he heard him babbling something about Wilton Knight being a "pioneer," "bucking the system" and some nonsense about the "American dream." All of this brilliant copy was rendered in an appropriately hushed tone of reverence.

Michael recorded one salient fact from the cliché-ridden hyperbole of the TV journalist— that Wilton Knight had been eighty-one years old at the time of his death. Elementary arithmetic confirmed a personal suspicion of Michael's: that Knight had been approximately his own age in 1934, when the first rumblings of the war were still distant and the country was still reeling from the Great Depression. That was when Knight had ceased being concerned solely with making money and empire building and begun to function in accordance with his personal ethic of individuality. Devon had sketched in Knight's background for Michael earlier; he knew, for example, that Knight had made and lost his first million as early as 1923.

And Michael had already guessed that it had been cancer, consuming Knight in a raging, internal conflagration. Knight had been suffering incredible levels of pain nearly the whole time he had interacted with Michael—he had believed *that* fervently in his plan.

Devon hurriedly tossed a white rose onto the already inundated silver casket and rushed to catch up with Michael. When he was within earshot he called out, "Michael—don't walk so fast. I'm not as spry as I used to be."

"Sorry, Devon—I've got places to go." To

Michael's mind, there was another line of expense on the bill run up by Tanya Walker, and it was time to collect.

"Yes, and things to do, and in your typically young, headstrong way you plan to begin this minute, without the faintest clue where to begin." He tucked his tall frame into the berth of the limousine next to Michael, and their uniformed driver pulled the long car out of the row and made for the cemetery gates.

"Take us back to the estate," Devon told the driver.

"There were at least four people involved in the ripoff at the casino," said Michael. "Tanya. Fred Wilson, Acton's security chief. A hit man—I saw him at Tres Piedras, a goon in a monkey suit. And a woman. Muntzy knew about the woman. They can't all have vanished without a trace. I have a better idea of where to start looking for them than you, Devon."

"Oh, do you?"

"Do you know something you're not telling me."

"A few things," Devon said airily. "Tanya is working in Silicon Valley. A town called Millston. She's already infiltrated another company called Com Tron. Perhaps 'infiltrated' is the wrong word. Com Tron seems to be her nest, her lair, the interest she's working for."

"The only interest Tanya works for is herself. Nobody owns or controls her."

"Quite. She's managed to slide herself into a position as executive assistant to William

Benjamin, the president of Com Tron. We're not sure if Com Tron is behind her espionage activities or not. Com Tron may only be her next target. With the right secrets and designs, an industrial spy could do quite well as a lone-wolf operative, selling to the highest bidder, without organizational backing."

"I know Silicon Valley. The area about a hundred miles north of Los Angeles. Where they make all the microchips."

"It's probably the wealthiest four-mile strip of space-age industry in the country," clarified Devon. "I'll wager that whatever she and her cohorts liberated from Charles Acton and Consolidated Chemical probably had the same applications to microchip technology as the secrets she helped to steal from Knight Industries a few years back."

"I thought scientists didn't wager, Devon."

Devon colored quickly. "What I meant was, she appears to be escalating her activities."

"She's still playing the same game," said Michael. "And if she's playing it in Silicon Valley, then that's where I'm headed—today."

"There you go again. I forbid you to leave so soon."

"*Forbid?* Wait just a second. Nobody owns or controls *me*, either, Devon! I'll climb out of this limo right now!"

"It would be in your best interests not to. I'll take away the car."

"You sound like my guardian telling me I can't go out on a date. To hell with the car. I'll get another one. Besides—it's registered in my name. It's still my property no matter what you did to it."

Tolerantly, Devon said, "That's where you're wrong." He pulled a leather billfold from his inside coat pocket, dropped it open, extracted a sheet of paper and handed it over.

Michael looked up from the registration slip. "Michael . . . *Knight*?"

"I keep telling you, Michael Arthur *Long* is long dead. And Arthur seems an appropriate middle name for a Knight, don't you think?"

"Ho, ho, ho, Devon," said Michael without inflection. "A barrel of laughs."

"You don't want to die laughing with the wrong name, do you? To die as Michael Long a second time?" Devon was completely serious. He gave the whole billfold to Michael.

"Dying once was enough, thank you." He examined the wallet and its contents, freezing momentarily with surprise. "Holy . . . driver's license, a Social Security number . . . petroleum cards, VISA, Mastercharge . . . Diner's Club . . . American Express Gold Card . . ." He thumbed back a stack of one-hundred-dollar bills in the cash pocket.

"All in the name of Michael Knight," said Devon. "All according to Wilton Knight's strict orders."

They were pulling into the broad cul-de-sac in front of the Knight mansion. Michael had his door open before the limousine came to a full stop. The Knight 2000 was parked nearby in the drive, waiting.

"In that case," said Michael, "as you've

thoughtfully equipped me with an identity *and* a destination, I'll be on my way."

Devon leapt from the limousine. "No! There are countless other things about the Knight 2000 that I haven't explained yet!"

Michael opened the pilot-side door and said, "Don't worry. I'm a pretty fast study. I'll pick things up as I go along."

"It's foolhardy and unwarranted!" Devon declared petulantly, his arms akimbo like an angry child's.

"Good-bye, Devon," Michael said from the window. "And thank you. I want you to know that I've kind of gotten to like you."

An incredulous expression crossed over Devon's face. "What?"

"Never mind. What does it mean, anyway, coming from a throwback like me; foolhardy and unwarranted . . . just like Wilton Knight in his more adventuresome days."

Devon's mouth was agape. "But—"

"Take it easy, Devon," Michael said and did one of the few things he felt comfortable doing in the frighteningly sophisticated Knight 2000: he floored the gas pedal, and roared away in a hail storm of spun gravel.

Devon stared after him.

Soon after Michael crossed the state line into California, a mileage sign shot past on Michael's right.

SAN FRANCISCO 241 mi./385.6 km.

MILLSTON 171 mi./273.6 km.

Highway 80 was deserted at midafternoon,

and Michael found nothing to do except gobble up the road and marvel at the complex control panels before him. He had not dared to switch the car into its unnerving AUTO CRUISE mode again, and uneasily wondered what might happen if he punched in the PURSUIT mode.

The dash, he decided, was needlessly complicated. *Over*complicated. He scanned in frustration the indicators, which possessed the same functions as a normal automobile, yet whose configurations were altered into incomprehensibility, making the whole dash alien. To the left of the AUTO CRUISE, lightbar there were signal bulbs reading AIR and OIL. He had gotten the meaning of the primary row of red neon digits by process of elimination—the speedometer. Other numbers allowed him to deduce specific, familiar functions, but most of the rest was still a mystery. He began to regret leaving Devon behind. There was not even a recognizable radio or tape deck to drive the silence back a bit.

"With all these stupid gadgets," Michael mused to himself, "you'd think they'd stick in a radio. Or an eight-track."

A modulated, even voice came in response: *"What would you like to hear? A little Beethoven, perhaps?"*

Michael nearly lost control of the car. But then, Devon had claimed even that was impossible.

The dash remained implacable except for a blinking yellow button bearing the acronym

KITT. He stabbed the button and the light ceased blinking, staying full on.

"Thank you," came the voice in response. *"Perhaps you'd prefer something more baroque. Bach, possibly."* Instantly the same prelude and fugue to which Wilton Knight had listened in the lab floated out from concealed speakers, filling the cockpit of the car.

"Stop it!" Michael shouted, and the song quit obligingly. "I want to know what the hell's going on? Devon? Is that you? Is this some kind of demented CB joke?"

"Mr. Knight, there is no need for increased volume. My audio sensors are tuned to discrete tolerances, and I am receiving your interrogatives with exceptional clarity. So please do not shout. In answer to your question, I am the technological voice of the Knight Industries 2000 microprocessor. My abbreviated designation is KITT, *for Knight Industries Two Thousand. You may prefer using the simple acronym,* KITT." Helpfully, the voice added, *"It's more familiar."*

"I do not prefer," snorted Michael. He finally noticed that the light red indicator screen just above the light bars on the steering column flashed whenever the voice spoke, like a light organ. He could not pick out the source of the sound itself; it seemed to issue from all around him inside the car. "And what's more I do *not* intend to ride around inside a car that talks back to me. So just give Devon a buzz and have yourself put on hold . . . or find yourself another driver."

"Unfortunately, Mr. Knight, I am not pro-

grammed to overrule your wishes even if they are in the form of directives."

"Oh, that's grand. That's real good to hear. Because I don't want to hear another peep out of you until I can fire off a call to Devon and get you neutralized. So clam up."

"As you wish, Mr. Knight."

Michael muttered to himself. "I'll pick my own damn . . . hey, wait a minute. Does this thing have a radio?" No response. "Did you hear me? Hello?"

The Knight Industries Two Thousand comes fully equipped," returned the voice laconically. It seemed to have a slight Boston accent, and reminded Michael of the fussy, peevish tone an East Coast movie critic might have. *"You'll find the proper buttons next to the infraray phasing controls, just under the microwave jammers and the readout table for the vital-signs scanner."*

"Can you give me that in English?"

"The unit next to your right knee, Mr. Knight."

"Thank you. Now shut up." The appropriate panel was conveniently blinking so Michael could locate it, and when he punched a toggle, a digital readout for the radio frequency popped on, with smaller, yellowish letters reading FM below it. He kept the toggle depressed and the numbers advanced.

"May I suggest that we put the vehicle into the AUTO CRUISE *mode for safety's sake?"* said the voice.

"Why?"

"I sense we are in a slightly irritable mood. Fatigue is the apparent cause."

"No, you may not suggest anything," Michael snapped, annoyed. And irritated. "That's final; now *good night*!"

"Good night."

"I can't believe this," Michael said under his breath. "Damned car starts talking to me; telling me what to do. This machine has got to go."

He finally located a rural station putting out the strains of the Rolling Stones and let the car fill up with the pumping rhythm of "Heartbreaker."

The sun dropped toward the horizon and eventually sank into the ocean Michael knew lay due west, somewhere over the peaks that blocked the view. The varicolored readout screens glowed in the darkness and made electronic light patterns on his face. The music had diminished to a background buzz, and more than once he found himself jerking his head suddenly up and refocusing his eyes on the road. The physical fatigue KITT had spoken of, the rigors of the last few days and of attending Wilton Knight's funeral on no sleep whatsoever, was beginning to make inroads on his consciousness.

Involuntarily, his head ducked again. He patted his cheek with increasing force until his vision cleared. When that failed, he bit down on his tongue.

Only a few more miles now. . . .

He put his head back against the brown plush head rest. That felt much more comfortable.

Michael's eyelids closed and stayed down.

He never saw the vital signs monitor come to life. Thin green lines traced his heart rate, brain waves, pulse and respiration, and microprocessors deduced that Michael was entering a sleep state in less than a quarter second.

The NORMAL CRUISE bar winked off and was replaced by the bright violet of the AUTO CRUISE mode. Michael's hands still hung, unfeeling, on the wheel.

KITT easily negotiated a mountain curve with no help at all from Michael.

About fifteen minutes later, KITT's sensors scanned the vehicle approaching from the rear. The information sped through the logic systems, and an instant later the red neon speedometer recorded a speed drop. The black street machine pulled slightly to the right to allow the approaching car to pass safely.

Inside the oncoming highway patrol cruiser, Officer Kyle glanced to the right as they passed the only other car on the road. He and Officer Deke Bannerman were making smoke to answer a call that had come in concerning a two-car smashup on one of the rural branch roads outside of Millston.

"Hey, Deke." Kyle tapped his fellow patrolman. "That boy's plumb asleep at the wheel."

Bannerman checked and saw Michael's head snuggled against the driver's window and the wheel apparently moving itself.

"Well, hit the horn. Get his attention."

Bannerman dropped speed until they were

running parallel to the black car, and Kyle hit the woop-woop siren once. No results. Bannerman honked the horn. Kyle gave the black racer another blast on the siren, this one longer.

Within the soundproofed interior of KITT, Michael remained peacefully oblivious, snoring.

"Oh, God—" blurted Kyle, eyes front.

Bannerman, who was driving but watching the next car, swung his eyes back onto the road in time to see a hairpin turn in the mountain road welling up at them. Beyond the worn white safety railing there was a two-hundred-foot drop terminating in a bowllike valley filled with fallen boulders and rocks eroded away from the cliff side across the road. Locally, the hairpin was known as Dead Man's Curve because of the many drunks that had been less than successful at navigating it.

Both the black car and the cruiser were right on top of it. Bannerman stood on the brakes and fishtailed the cruiser hard to the left to avoid smacking into the flimsy guard-rail. Kyle let out a yell of fear.

The cruiser ground, shuddering, to a smoky halt as both officers watched the black car negotiate the curve perfectly.

"I thought that boy was deader'n a door-nail!" said Kyle. "Jeez! I guess he woke up just in time."

"Woke up nothing," Bannerman growled, angry now. "We got us a bomber pilot tonight, Kyle—probably snockered and playing footsie with the big bad coppers. Let's go get him!" Deke mashed the pedal down and spun the cruiser around, digging out with a great deal of smoke and noise. Kyle put the flash bar on, and the red and blue lights lit up the black car's rear deck.

KITT decreased the volume on the radio and commenced a wakeup pager, beeping at two per second, until Michael's alpha-wave pattern registered an oscillation. He was waking up.

He rubbed his eyes, and the first thing he saw was the police car.

"Oh, no." He yawned. "What did I do?"

"Deny everything," said KITT.

Michael changed the dashboard setting from AUTO to NORMAL CRUISE and took the wheel, steering to the skinny shoulder of the mountain road and stopping. The highway patrol car angled diagonally across his path, preventing further progress, and the driver, a large officer tending a bit to fat, unhorsed himself and strode toward KITT as his partner stood ready behind him, his hand on his hip. If they were angry enough to draw their guns, Michael thought, this could be touchy.

"May I suggest that deafness is usually a prudent approach to employ with law-enforcement officers?"

"Quiet; I'll take care of this," said Michael. "Your buggy little computer brain was probably making the car weave all over the road."

"On the contrary. You couldn't have driven better. I might additionally suggest you conspic-

*uously display a slight kink in your neck, since
you were supposedly 'driving' with your head
propped against the window."*

"That's just stupendous. Why didn't you
warn me like you're supposed to?"

*"You disallowed it. I believe you instructed
me to SHUT UP."*

Michael was taken aback by the last two
words, which came in his own voice—a recording, played back for his benefit.

"Who's that boy talkin' to?" Kyle said
warily, looking the car up and down.

"He ain't talking to nobody," Deke said,
annoyed with his partner. "He's talkin' to his
CB. Or he's talkin' to himself since he's probably drunk as a skunk. Come on." He thumped
on the hood of the car. "Let's go, boy, drag it
out of the car and let's get it over with!"

Michael rolled down the pilot window but
did not get out of the car.

"Say," said Deke. "You're comin' out or
you're spendin' a night in the bullpen, you
read me, boy?"

Michael innocently moved his lips without
emitting any sound, and pointed exaggerat-
edly to his ears.

"You got the balloon, Kyle?"

"I'M SORRY, OFFICER," Michael said,
enunciating over carefully and too loudly.
"BUT CAN YOU ... SPEAK IN SIGN LAN-
GUAGE ... OR SLIGHTLY SLOWER? I'M
AFRAID I ... HAVEN'T QUITE GOTTEN LIP
READING ... DOWN YET."

"He can't hear?" said Kyle with a bewildered look.

Michael made several meaningless signatory motions with one hand to confuse them even more, then bellowed, "COULD YOU TALK LOUDER . . . INTO THIS EAR?" He indicated his left ear.

Kyle still had not figured out what was happening. "You mean you're deaf?" he said, and then backed up a step, as if the condition might be contagious.

Deke cocked his Smoky Bear hat back. "I guess that explains everything. Nobody drunk could drive so smooth, but he couldn't hear us."

"WHAT . . .?" shouted Michael.

Kyle leaned down and yelled into Michael's face with broad, overplayed lip movements. "HE SAID . . . THAT YOU'RE . . . DEAF, SO WE . . ."

"Never mind, Kyle," said Deke, clearly fed up. He walked back to the cruiser.

"SORRY TO BOTHER YOU," continued Kyle. "WATCH YOUR REARVIEW MIRROR!" He pointed so Michael would get the idea. "WE'VE BEEN FLASHING YOU FOR MILES!"

"YES SIR!" shouted Michael. "I'LL DO THAT! THANKS, OFFICER!"

He watched them climb back into their cruiser and go. His shoulders slumped in relief. "Why do I get this feeling that this won't be the last time I run into trouble in this place?" Quickly he glared at KITT's red speaker screen. "Don't answer that."

"Yes sir."

Just past the bend in the road Michael passed a scenic green sign that read: WELCOME TO MILLSTON/CITY LIMITS.

And just beyond that was a huge billboard displaying a convoluted corporate logo.

"Com Tron," said Michael as he drove into the town.

5

Millston's main drag was overwhelmed by the Com Tron manufacturing plant on the right side of the two-stoplight street and the support facilities—mostly bars and restaurants—on the opposite side. One side of the Com Tron plant was entirely painted over with a huge, outlandish mural depicting a rolling pasture with grazing cattle. The leg of the plant Michael could see from the intersection covered at least four city blocks.

The stoplight changed to green and Michael cruised the street. There seemed to be Com Tron logos on everything; he even spotted a company store. Then everything else was drowned out by a bright, flashing marquee that momentarily reminded Michael of the million-bulb signs in the casinos of Vegas and Reno.

"House of the Rising Sun," read Michael.

"That was a song by the Animals back in the 1960s, if I remember correctly."

"Actually, it was first performed by Miriam Makeba for the Letters label, in America. It's an African tune. . . ."

Michael ignored the car. Secondary neon signs winked furiously on and off, proclaiming such diversions as a sushi/sashimi bar, disco dancing nightly, ladies' night, special prices on well drinks, Beer Night, mud wrestling and wet T-shirt competitions every Saturday and—Michael blinked—*hotel accommodations?*

"This looks like a good place to start sniffing around," he said. He had acquired the nearly unconscious habit of speaking to the machine as though it were a human passenger. He rationalized this by pretending he was speaking to himself to keep from being driven crazy by the concept of a machine that might be able to outthink him, and was a smart aleck to boot. "If the local scene starts anywhere, it starts here."

"Saloons are conducive to 'scenes,' as you call them," said KITT.

"How would you know?" Michael grabbed an empty parking slot to the left of the glittering marquee.

"Social gathering places where both sexes have the free option of mingling and consuming large quantities of alcoholic beverages create an environment where indiscretion becomes commonplace," droned KITT. *"Just remember this is business, not pleasure."*

Michael could not take it anymore, and pushed the door open violently to avoid punching out the expensive dash. "You can say that again, Frankenstein!" he shouted. "You're about as much fun as a root canal! Or a Reno divorce—which is getting to sound like a pretty good idea!"

Three women standing near the entrance of the House of the Rising Sun had stopped talking and turned to take note of Michael's outburst.

"*I want custody of me, in that event,*" said KITT.

Michael slammed the door, then kicked it, hard. Not a scratch was left on the diamond-hard black surface. "Damn!" He stormed toward the entrance. "Miserable thing . . . should have yanked your vocal wires or something! Now I can't shut you up! Nag, nag, nag!"

He looked up and saw that the three ladies were staring at him as though the Creature from the Black Lagoon had just sauntered up wearing an ascot and a cowboy hat.

"Ah—evening, ladies," he said, and hurried past them into the lounge.

They all looked to each other, their general reaction best described by a finger pointed at the temple and moved in a circle. "Some guys sure start hitting the juice early," one of them said.

The speaker turned and nodded toward the Com Tron plant gate across the street. She was no longer clad in the butterfly-thin blue evening dress. Tonight Lonnie was wearing skintight designer jeans and was braless beneath a very sheer silk blouse the color of a fresh plum. The unbuttoned top three buttons were good strategy. Thin strands of gold accented both her neck and her tan. Her spangled earrings glistened inside the forest of rich brunette hair. She directed her two partners, equally attractive, equally dressed to kill, toward the trio of business-suited young men just coming through the Com Tron security gate. They girded themselves for the coming confrontation.

"I know they aren't as pretty as the guy that just walked in," said Lonnie, "but these guys are our problem and the space case isn't. Just remember that. Stick to business, ladies, at least for tonight. Sally, get inside and grab a booth for us."

Sally complied. She was wearing a close-fitting hot-pink jumpsuit littered with golden zippers, the center one having given as much ground as the buttons on Lonnie's blouse.

"Okay, they've spotted us," said Lonnie. "Let's get inside."

From his position in a corner booth, Michael saw the women file in and immediately recognized the earmarks of a setup. He shook his head slowly as the group of six crowded into the booth, with as much physical contact as possible. Those Com Tron guys never had a chance, he mused: the women were pretty stunning.

He stuck to beer, biding his time and watching. It seemed to be the first time he'd had to

himself since the night Muntzy had been killed;
the first time he'd been shut of the circus at
the Knight estate. It occurred to him that he
was sitting, drinking and watching women for
the first time in ages, and he took solace in
the fact that one of the trio he'd passed
outside kept glancing back at him from the
booth across the room. The one in the pink
jumpsuit and knee-high boots. They were all
attractive, to be sure, he thought—but they
were all black-widow types.

The House of the Rising Sun was rolling
with business. Loud, attractive couples and
foursomes strove to be witty while waiting
for their sandwiches and steak platters. Clots
of men were being raucously chauvinistic at
the long, horseshoe-shaped bar, checking out
the flesh parade and nodding grunts of approval. Blue-collar types in work shirts and
heavy-equipment baseball caps worked on
their reserved and powerful drinks, occasionally arm-wrestling or weaving back to the bar
for another full pitcher like sailboats in a
squall. Groups of women mirrored the actions of the bunches of girl-watching men.
Com Tron gambits were laid by young, wildly
gesturing executives in one booth, while in
the next an assignation was planned by a
just-introduced couple with dark, hopeful eyes.
Everyone moved through their special ritual
dances, and Michael watched them all. His
empty beer mug was replaced by a full. KITT
had been right about the environment.

Inside the booth across from Michael's calm

corner, things grew more relevant as the evening wore on. The woman in the plum blouse, the brunette, converted her motion of reaching for a vodka collins glass into a covert nibble on the earlobe of the Com Tron executive seated next to her. Beneath the booth, his hand had already made acquaintance with her thigh. The third girl exchanged a "friendly" kiss with her date. The woman in the pink jumpsuit kept glancing—unobtrusively, she thought—back toward Michael. She laughed and nodded and played along enthusiastically, but did not get as physical as her two partners.

Michael's mug was replenished again, and a voice said, "Your tab's starting to climb, my friend. Or are you our charity drinker this week? You don't look broke."

Michael broke off his eye contact with the woman in the pink jumpsuit as the cocktail waitress hefted his dry mug. She was a petite blond woman Michael estimated to be in her late twenties, attractive but not overpoweringly so. Perhaps she only appeared plain in comparison to the superfoxes across the room. Her eyes were not as empty or conniving as theirs.

"Oh, sure." Michael dug for his wallet. Stenciled over the waitress's left breast pocket was the name *Maggie* in yellow embroidery. "Say, Maggie . . . do you know who those people in the corner booth are?"

She gave them the briefest of glances and grew defensive. "Let me do you a favor. My good deed for the day to a stranger. Don't get interested in anybody at that booth no matter how luscious they look. They're poison. Mix with them and you'll wake up with your teeth in the dirt—if you wake up at all."

"I'm not interested in them specifically," said Michael with a winning smile. The waitress reciprocated, pleased with the attention. "I noticed outside that they all came from Com Tron."

"So?"

"So, I'm trying to look up an old friend of mine who works for Com Tron."

"I used to work at Com Tron," said Maggie. "Most of the faces are familiar to me. A lot of them are regulars here. This friend of yours—what's his name?"

"It's not a him, it's a her. Tanya Walker."

Maggie's smile solidified, then vanished. Her eyes turned steely. She lifted a fresh mug of beer off the tray crooked against her arm and dumped the foaming contents into Michael's lap.

"*Hey!*" yelled Michael, trying to stand but blocked by the narrow booth. "What's the matter wi—"

"Take that to Tanya Walker, hot pants."

Everyone in the lounge was suddenly very interested, and very quiet. The mustachioed bartender got across the room in a hurry with a towel, mopping theatrically at Michael, who pushed his eagerly offered help away. "Terrible accident," he fawned. "I *am* so sorry, sir, of course we'll pay the cleaning costs . . . and you can have another on the house. . . ."

"No accident, George," said Maggie.

"What?" Realization hit the bartender. "Dammit, Maggie, this is this last straw! I'm not putting up with your discourtesy to our guests any longer! Punch your card, now— don't even finish up here, I'll do it. You're fired!" The little man was still fussing over Michael's clothing.

Michael stood up at last, beer soaking his jeans and leather jacket. "Look, that's not necessary . . . we just had a little misunder-standing. . . ."

"Shut up, you jerk!" Maggie shouted. "Un-derstand this! I fight my own battles! Go hang out with your slimy Com Tron buddies!" She shoved her full tray into George the bartender's midriff. He overbalanced and came forward, spilling four more full mugs of beer all over himself and Michael.

Maggie stalked off, ripping away her vinyl apron and flinging it grandly across the bar. Several people applauded, mockingly. She crashed through the swinging kitchen doors and was gone.

Michael angled around George, wiping splat-ters of beer from his face. "No offense, George, but I think I'll leave before I become a total sponge. I smell like a frat house already."

He made a point of tipping an imaginary hat across the bar to Sally, the woman in the jumpsuit, before he left. She was watching him very closely.

Outside, a voice stopped him before he could get back to his car.

"Hey!"

Michael turned and saw the leader of the trio, the striking woman in the plum blouse. He stood there pointing at himself, mouthing *who, me?* as she stepped from the doorway and caught up with him.

"I heard you mention Tanya Walker," she said breathlessly, brushing back her hair and giving Michael a good, long look. "You a friend of hers?"

"That depends on whether you've got a mugful of beer in your hand," said Michael.

She rolled her eyes. "I'm unarmed. You can search me if you want. I'm not going to toss anything at you; Tanya's a compadre of mine, too."

Michael was still brushing drops of beer from his jacket. Lonnie held up a handful of bar napkins and he accepted them gratefully. "Do you know how I might get in touch with her?"

"I'm afraid Tanya is already seeing someone. She's seriously involved." Lonnie took a napkin and wiped off Michael's shoulders and blotted his back.

"I'm not that kind of friend," Michael said. "I'm interested in her pocketbook, not her wonderful body."

"Come again?"

"I have some merchandise to sell. I think Tanya'll be interested. I decided to come to her first; give her first crack at buying it."

"Like what kind of merchandise?"

Michael looked around. He and Lonnie were

alone in the parking lot. "Like that's between me and Tanya, and only if she's interested. Can you help me or not?"

Lonnie pursed her frosted lips in thought, then said, "Who shall I tell her is inquiring?"

"Tell her it's an old friend," Michael said, opening the car door. "Thanks for your help." He winked.

She smiled. "You're welcome." She watched the flowing black automobile back out and tool away.

Lonnie did not have to scribble down the license plate number. It was simple to remember. She logged it in her brain and hurried back to the bar to find a telephone.

The private extension rang twice, with that soft, burring ring characteristic of "enclosed" phone systems like those found in large hotels or office buildings. A gravelly voice answered. "Security. Symes here."

Tanya pictured Symes, who had overseen the incident at Tres Piedras, sitting at his ratty secondhand desk in his rumpled security uniform. His feet would be propped up on one of the drop leafs of the desk. Symes was not natty, but like Gray, Fred Wilson's number-one dirty-work man, Symes was good at what he did.

As for herself, Tanya preferred a touch more opulence. "This is Tanya. Someone just came into Millston asking around about Com Tron and about me specifically." She was speaking to the vox box on the wide expanse of desk in

front of her, and Symes's rough-edged voice
was coming out of the speaker phone next to
it. "No name, but let me give you a license
number to run down." She described the car
as Lonnie had described it to her. "Nevada
license, by the way. A vanity plate with the
letters K-N-I-G-H-T. That should be easy
enough to spot."

"Like a flasher at a grade-school playground,"
said Symes. "If it's a cop, he sure doesn't like
keeping a low profile. I'll check it. If it *is* a
cop, we'll handle him like we did the last
ones."

Tanya smiled to herself. "Symes, you read
my mind." She punched the disconnect just
as she heard the door to the plush Com Tron
office thump shut.

"Who're you calling, love?" came Will Benjamin's voice. He rounded the foyer corner, a
large man in his mid-forties with the ramrod-
straight spine and self-conscious posture of a
man who was both a decorated military vet-
eran and a successful corporate wrangler.

Tanya stood and turned into Benjamin's
broad embrace. His arms wrapped around
her and cinched tight; then they both backed
up for a deep kiss. "I was just talking to our
security people," Tanya said. "As president of
Com Tron, you're an irreplaceable asset—as
the accounting boys would say—and I want
to make sure you'll be safe during the ruckus
tomorrow. You know how I worry about you
out in public, darling." Tanya was displaying

exactly the same concern she had displayed with Charles Acton only a few weeks ago.

"Nothing's going to happen to me," Benjamin said gruffly.

"Ah, but in this day and age . . . who knows? There are all kinds of unscrupulous people who'd like to get their hands on a man representative of as much power and money as you. Extremists. Terrorists. Extortionists. Leftwingers. Any man as far ahead as you is bound to attract them. . . ." She set his lapels and kept her eyes locked on his.

"Not to mention tax accountants, and charity folks, and newspaper reporters," Benjamin joked. He briefly considered the corporate litter on his desktop, shrugged and turned toward his private cocktail buffet to pour something stiff with a little ice.

Tanya moved to the overstuffed leather sofa, sat back, levered off her high heels and beckoned to him. Benjamin shrugged and brought along two drinks.

"Take off your coat and don't worry about the people who may or may not be out to get you," she said. "Just be grateful you have me to look out for your best interests."

She drew him down and planted her mouth firmly on his. Over his shoulder she watched the phone box. If a stranger was checking up on her, she wanted to know who it might be.

But first, she had other work to attend to.

6

Following a fast change into dry clothing,
Michael returned to the House of the Rising
Sun. This time he cruised the back alleyway
where the employees—and one ex-employee,
he hoped—parked their cars while on shift.

The deep crimson sensor in the hood of the
black car—the thing Michael had facetiously
called a "death ray"—scanned the parked cars
as Michael found an unobtrusive slot parallel
to the opposite alley wall and pulled into it.

*"Not having immediate access to the records
of the department of motor vehicles in this state,"*
said KITT, *"I'd estimate that the somewhat
delapidated old Volkswagen is the car you're
looking for. Based on purely circumstantial clues,
but logical deduction."*

"It's a relief to know you can't do everything," said Michael.

KITT clarified. *"I said I didn't have* immediate *access. A complete computer match via radiophone lines is in-work.*"

"That's okay, forget it," said Michael with a wave of his hand. "I figure it's Maggie's car, too."

"On what do you base this conclusion?"

Michael paused before answering, and finally, mostly to annoy KITT, he said, "Call it a hunch."

"I call it illogical."

"We both arrived at the same conclusion using different methods. That means one of us is redundant."

KITT had no comeback for that one, but Michael sensed the machine would not forget.

Michael spotted the slice of light from an opening door, then saw the security gate for the employee entrance to the bar swing open in the dark. Maggie came quickly out, lugging a cardboard boxful of odds and ends, most likely from her recently vacated locker. She paused to heave something into the trash dumpster, then balanced the box on one arm as she dug out the keys to the VW both Michael and KITT had settled on as being her car.

From the open window, Michael said, "Maggie . . ."

She spun around, dropping the box. Something broke with a tinkle when it hit the pavement. "Stay where you are, you creep!" she snarled. "I've got a canful of mace!"

"Maggie, it's Michael—the one you gave all

the free beer to. I stayed in my car so I wouldn't scare you."

She squinted toward the black car. "Fat lot of good it did," she said, stooping to retrieve her belongings. "My blouse fell in the mud, so you can stuff your continental manners, David Niven." She pawed around for her stuff and dropped her car keys in the alleyway. "Damn!"

Michael got out of his car to help, and she sprang back up. "Hey! I'm warning you, don't come any closer to me or I'll ruin your whole freaking *week*, bozo!" She had her mace canister poised.

"Listen," Michael said, hands extended to show he wasn't armed—or whatever Maggie expected. "I'm sorry about your job, and what happened inside awhile ago. But you misunderstood about Tanya Walker. I'm not looking for her because I just want to pay a social call."

"Who gives a damn? Not me." She located her keys, unlocked the Volkswagen and threw her stuff inside without bothering to repack the box. "Tanya Walker and her little group of vampires are behind the theft of everything *I* ever cared about: my husband, my house and now my job. Already I'm too broke to get my kid some decent clothes. So why don't you break my heart with your own little sob story!" She was close to tears and did not wish to break down in front of a stranger, and so climbed into her VW, slammed the door and started the engine. When she began to back out she saw that Michael's car left no room for turning around. "Get that machine out of my way, mister—or I'm going to put a hell of a dent in it. I mean it!" She revved her engine to emphasize her anger.

Michael shrugged. "Go ahead, be my guest, if it'll make you feel better. . . ."

From within the car KITT's voice said, *"That's easy for you to say—it's MY bodily abuse we're discussing here!"*

"You asked for it, you creep," Maggie said, popping her clutch and ramming Michael's car with the tail end of the VW.

The crash echoed in the alleyway. The VW stalled out just in time for Maggie to hear the clangor caused by her rear bumper falling off and ringing on the concrete. Michael was still standing in the same position as she jumped out and looked at the damage. There was not even a smudge on the portion of KITT that had received the hit.

Her arms dropped to her sides in resignation. "Today's really my day," she said wonderingly. "They put bumpers on these things to *prevent* damage, and mine drops off."

"I'm sorry," said Michael. "I'll pay to have it fixed for you."

Maggie pinched the bridge of her nose, as though she had a severe migraine headache. "Nobody has luck this bad."

"I can help you change your luck."

"Look, why don't you drift out of my life, huh? Leave me alone." She pointed at the bar's back door. "That was the last place I'll ever get a job in Millston. Everything just slid down the toilet as soon as you walked in."

"What if I told you that I'm here to run Tanya and her parasite club out of Millston?"

That caught her short. A laugh burst out of her and she looked at him from the corner of her eye. "Don't tell me. You're gonna hand me a silver bullet and Tonto is gonna climb out of that flashy black car."

"No. But I think I can give you a chance to get even."

"If I'll help you, is that it? Or is it something else you want?" What Michael was talking about seemed too good to come without conditions.

"Like I said in the bar, I need information. I'm still hoping you can tell me what I need to know. About Tanya and about Com Tron."

"I saw Lonnie chase you out of the bar," said Maggie accusingly. "I figured she just batted her eyelashes at you and you got what you wanted." There was a vague hint of jealousy in her voice.

"I think she'll pass the word on to Tanya that someone is looking for her," said Michael. "But Lonnie just looked like another of Tanya's black widows."

Maggie brightened, but was still studying him uncertainly. "How do I know you're not just another one of them?"

"You don't," responded Michael quickly. "And if I just blithely said I was, you wouldn't believe me. But I will offer you a lift home."

"I don't know how much I can help you; you might not get your money's worth."

"Let's find out. Either way I think I might gain a pretty valuable friend. And that's worth more than all the tight pink jumpsuits there are."

Maggie spanked her hands together and moved toward the passenger side of Michael's car. Of course, he added mentally, she wasn't bad-looking herself.

"They call this the Silicon Valley Strip," Maggie said, indicating the expanse of factories, nightclubs, restaurants and motels unfolding around them on the five-lane street. Lots of neon and wildly flashing lights moved by outside. "Millston is a regular boom town. There's more money flowing through here right now than there was on the whole coastline during the California Gold Rush."

"All thanks to microchips so small you can get them stuck between the grooves on your finger," said Michael. He thought that it was the same technology that had made an achievement like KITT possible. Maggie had given the car's somewhat flamboyant instruments a second and third glance as she rode, but did not mention it or ask about it.

"Yep. Every pocket calculator that plays 'Sweet Adeline,' every eighty-function wristwatch, every electronic kid's game, the guts of every home computer—they were all born right here."

"So how do you fit into Silicon Valley, Maggie?"

Her hands fidgeted in her lap. "My husband moved us here so he could take a position with Com Tron as head of their security branch."

"It obviously didn't work out."

"It did," she said with a grim expression, "until Benjamin—that's Will Benjamin, Com Tron's president—got himself a new executive assistant. Nobody could *believe* her. She started as a Girl Friday type, you know, fill-ins . . . and inside of three months she became Benjamin's private trouble-shooter and live-in mistress."

"I get three guesses who that was, right?" said Michael.

"Uh-huh," said Maggie, watching the lights. "Before Tanya Walker rode her flashy little tailfeathers to the top, Com Tron was a pretty jolly corporation. You might say she got to the top by starting on *her* bottom. It was after her so-called 'promotion' that the wholesale changes started."

"Starting with your husband?"

"Philip got fired, and I think it was because he was too honest. He came home and told me things: suspicions of high-level industrial espionage, theft of designs, that sort of thing. He wanted to get hardcore evidence to show to Will Benjamin personally. He used his knowledge of the plant and some contacts who were still his friends to try and collect that evidence. And then one night he didn't come home."

"He got caught."

"The highway patrol came to my house the next morning. His car was stuck in a gulley off Sunset Ridge Road and his neck was broken over the steering wheel. Half a dozen witnesses all swore to the accident. The cops said Philip had been drinking and ran off the road."

"That sounds a little too neat for the circumstances."

"The witnesses were all truck drivers owned by Com Tron. You saw some of them in the House of the Rising Sun; the guys in the Cat Man ball caps. What's more, Philip didn't drink—he never drank. Not even beer. Never." A green street sign appeared out of the night. They were well off the strip now. "Turn at the next right," she said.

"You wouldn't have taken that barmaid job for the same reasons your husband went sleuthing around the plant, now would you?"

She seemed to resent the obvious suggestion, which gave it a better than even chance of being true. "I took that scut job for one reason: to feed Buddy, our little boy. Pull over here." She gestured toward a duplex in the dark. "This is where I live now, on the other side of the Com Tron tracks. What else would you like to know?"

"Everything," said Michael.

Maggie was game enough. "In that case, you'd better come on in."

Maggie rapped hard on the front door, and presently there was the sound of various police locks being unbolted and security slide chains thrown back. An accented Hispanic voice said, "Ah, Maggie, we was beginning to wonder where you were." She pronounced it *MAH-gee*.

"Sorry I'm late, Luce, I ran into something—"

The door opened and a diminutive Mexican woman wearing jeans and a Mickey Mouse T-shirt saw Maggie under the porch light along with the taller figure behind her. "Well, I hope it was nothing seri— Oh! My! I hope it *is* something serious!" Luce's eyes scanned Michael up and down several times with obvious delight as the pair entered.

"Luce, please," Maggie said, embarrassed. "This is . . . Mr. uh, Knight? Mr. Knight."

Michael bowed with a little smile, and Luce was more than pleased to meet him.

"Luce watches after Buddy," Maggie said.

Luce was all smiles. "But not when Buddy's mom is around," she added. "He is asleep now. And I'm leaving." She swept a couple of shopping bags into her arms. "Have a good time, you two—you especially, Margarita." To Michael she said, "I am pleased to meet you, Mr. Knight, and I will tell you that this is a wonderful woman. A saint. Remember that." She hugged Maggie good-bye for the evening despite her double armload of bags, and whispered *"buena suerte"* when they were close— good luck.

Then, like a miniature whirlwind, she was gone.

"That's quite a housekeeper you've got there," said Michael. Maggie's apartment was neat, clean and cheap.

"Oh, Luce's not anybody's housekeeper. She doesn't do windows. She just takes care of Buddy." She kept her face averted, but Michael could see she was blushing furiously. She faced him, saying, "I don't know what to tell you; Luce *never* acts like that!"

"No apologies necessary," said Michael. "What could I be but flattered?"

"You have to understand," she said, sitting down. "I haven't . . . I haven't had a man in my apartment since Philip—"

"Mom . . .?" Behind the soft, sleepy voice came a small, sleepy boy of eight or nine, wearing E.T. pajamas with feet.

"I'll bet this is Buddy," said Michael.

"What on earth are you doing still up?"

"I heard ya come in, Mom." Buddy looked up at Michael. "Hi! You gonna marry my mom?"

Maggie's mouth unhinged and locked in the open position.

"*Now* you really have to hit the sack, big guy!"

Dutifully, Buddy padded across the kitchen. "G'night, Mom," he said, pecking Maggie on the cheek. Then he promptly raided the refrigerator, quickly chugging some milk and stowing away two chocolate-chip cookies before Maggie rose and ushered him back to his room. "Right back to bed with you ... will you excuse me a minute, Michael?"

"Sure. I know you've probably got to get some sleep yourself, so I'll try not to take up too much time." A light came on down the short hallway and Michael idled around the compact living room. Pictures of Buddy and his dad stood on a wrought-iron shelf. "Where's the best place to get ahold of Tanya?" he called down the hall. "Com Tron? Does she have a place in town?"

Buddy's voice, muffled, came from his bedroom: "Who's Tanya—the competition?"

"You hush and get in bed!" came Maggie's voice. Buddy's light went out and the door closed. "Forget trying to see her off duty. And she's usually attached to Will Benjamin. She lives at his estate now. But they both have to appear in public tomorrow." She came back out into the living room wearing a loose-fitting chambray shirt with the sleeves rolled up instead of her work blouse. "Com Tron is sponsoring a charity race out at the track, and as president and owner, Benjamin has to oversee it."

"The track?"

"It used to be a dirt-bike dragway. The event Com Tron sponsors is a demolition derby, with the gate receipts going to disease-research charities. The gimmick is that all the entries are brand-new late model cars; they don't use junkers. It's like conspicuous consumption on a Roman-arena scale. The locals eat it up." She made a pallid try at lightheartedness:

"Say, maybe I could go down there after the race and find a new bumper, you know, from all the debris? Nah. They never enter anything as cheap as a VW."

"You mean anybody can enter? It's not just confined to the corporation?" Michael had the germ of an idea.

"Sure, I suppose . . . but who's crazy enough to want to enter a car fresh off the showroom floor into a smash festival like that? Anyway, it was Buddy who wanted to go, not me."

"Fine. I'll pick you both up at ten sharp."

"What? You mean you want to see this thing?"

"You two can watch," Michael said, his inner gears cranking away. You can watch *me*. I think I might be crazy enough to enter. . . ."

Like a jack-in-the-box, Buddy's head poked out of his bedroom doorway long enough for him to voice his approval: "Yeah! All right!"

The door slammed as Michael and Maggie regarded each other with uneasy smiles.

The Newtown Dirt Racing Center also had a baseball diamond tucked off to one side like a homy, small-town park. Michael reflected that most of the hi-tech Silicon Valley townships had sleepy, unobtrusive names, as though they were nothing more than rural bedroom communities: Millston, Newtown, Lewisville, Connard, Downey Corners. But all the shining hardware in evidence at the race track gave the lie to the idea of drowsy little burgs that would evade the notice of passers-through, which was exactly how the corporations over-lording the towns liked it. Loitering near the start-flag line were several gleaming, sleek automobiles newly minted from Detroit. Their fenders and door panels were plastered with foil decals that caught and reflected the sun-light, the convoluted corporate logos of the individual sponsors who had donated the cars to the cause. Service teams in brightly col-ored jumpers swarmed around more entrants, rolling parts and testing equipment from im-posing Com Tron trucks. Michael now no-ticed that each car, although bearing the standards of individual companies, all had a Com Tron label and stripes dominating its rear fenders. Michael circled the track once on the access road, outside the rails and walls, just to get an overview of the entire setup. He hoped KITT was paying attention to all that was going on.

"Wow!" declared Buddy, leaning forward from the backseat to gape. "It's better than the dune buggy and dirt-bike show!"

"Better admire 'em while you can, kiddo," said Maggie. "Because there isn't going to be much left of them in about an hour and a half. . . ." Maggie was radiant today, inside of a checked shirt tied off at the midriff and revealing a flat, muscular tummy and cutoffs that showed off her supple legs.

Michael approved. "Why all the trucks from Com Tron?" he said, pointing. They were all over the track, servicing every entry in the race.

"Com Tron sponsors the race, so Com Tron provides the drivers. They're all professionals. You may have noticed these things aren't as well built as race cars, so there's an element of risk." She ran a finger along KITT's smooth dash with regret. "You're really not thinking of entering your beautiful set of wheels, are you? Those Com Tron goons will make scrap metal out of it."

Buddy, who clearly approved, made a violent car-crash noise. "Wipe out!"

"What the heck," said Michael. "It's for charity, isn't it? We've all got to do our bit."

"It's also for people who can afford to throw money away." Clearly this offended her frugal sensibilities. "I can't figure out why *you're* doing it. You're not like them."

"I have my reasons. You'll see. Don't worry."

"You're a strange man, Michael Knight. With a strange, improbable name. Nice—but strange."

"Thank you, ma'am," he said with cowboy gallantry that made her laugh. "Now let's check in and find you guys some seats in the owner's row."

Maggie turned. "Me, in the owner's row?" Then she sat back in her seat with satisfaction. "That'll frost 'em!"

He dropped them off to wander around for a few minutes, while he concentrated on his first confrontation with his objective: Tanya Walker, seated with several other women at the credentials booth. He had the advantage of a face she would not recognize as he approached the booth.

"I understand this is where I check in ... Tanya."

Tanya shaded her eyes from the sunlight and looked up. She was wearing a leather outfit with a blazing red scarf around her neck that floated in the light breeze. "I beg your pardon ... have we met?"

Michael's eyes, the only physical feature that might betray him, were hidden by his bronze racing glasses. "I'm Michael Knight."

"Oh, the man on the telephone this morning. Is that your car? You mean you were serious about entering it in our little local competition here?" The other women had piped down and were now watching the confrontation between Tanya and the stranger in the jeans and the black leather jacket.

"Dead serious," said Michael.

Tanya lifted a clipboard and shot through some of the rules. "Your car serves as the entry fee," she clarified. "If I were you, I wouldn't plan on getting too much of it back. First prize is a trophy and five thousand dollars. A lot of the drivers are pros, and eager for that five grand."

"If I win, I'll give the prize money to whatever charity Com Tron is supporting."

"Pretty generous," Tanya said. "Pretty confident. What if you get written off along with your car? This can get pretty scary sometimes. Dangerous for semipros."

"These days, Tanya, what isn't risky and

dangerous?" He smiled and her expression stayed frozen. "By the way—has anyone mentioned to you that I was in town?"

"As a matter of fact, yes. But I didn't understand the message." Pointedly, she added, "And I don't deal with salesmen."

"Not even when they haven't told you what they're selling yet?"

"It doesn't matter," she said. The implication was clear: she could have almost whatever could be bought, hers for the asking.

Michael made to leave. "You're wrong. After the race you'll be looking for me—I guarantee it."

"Mr.—ah, Knight. I'm not sure we can accept such an unauthorized entry into this race. At least, not without proper credentials." She put down the clipboard and stood up, all business and without humor. "Why are you here? And where are you from?" She studied him closely. "And who the hell *are* you? Have we met before? And if we haven't, why are you interested in me?"

As she turned, perhaps to signal someone in security, Will Benjamin came from behind the credentials booth, taking her arm. "Tanya—let's go. The crowd's waiting on us."

Before she could speak, Michael cut between them and snatched Benjamin's hand, pumping it vigorously up and down like a hungry politician, giving the corporate boss a smile very nearly the proverbial foot wide. "You *have* to be Mr. Benjamin! Just let me say that I sure do admire all the work you're doing on behalf of charity here, and I'm just pleased as punch to be doing my fair share!''

Benjamin, a man who went way back in the art of the handshake, returned the force of Michael's grip, pleased without really knowing why. ''Uh—doing your share? I'm afraid I don't—''

''Oh,'' Michael said. ''What I mean is I guess I'm the only independent driver in your race, here. But it's still an honor. Yes sir!''

Tanya stood on hold just behind Benjamin, who began to figure out what Michael's tirade of happy clichés meant. ''Your enthusiasm is just what we need, but I'm afraid we don't use junk stock cars in this kind of demo derby, Mr.—?''

''He says his name is Knight,'' said Tanya coldly.

''And my car's no jalopy, Mr. Benjamin. She's brand spankin' new and sitting right over there. See for yourself.''

''Oh,'' said Benjamin, looking over KITT's sleek lines. *''Oh!* Well, I trust Tanya here has explained the rules to you?''

''She's been quite helpful,'' Michael said, watching her from behind his glasses.

''Well, Mr. Knight, all I've got to say is you're a generous fellow, and welcome. Tanya, I want you to make sure that the crowd here knows about Mr. Knight's gesture and appreciates it, okay?''

Tanya remained calm, but her gaze at Michael was livid. ''Naturally.''

''And Miss Walker, I'll need my passes to

the owner's row now, please." Apparently
Tanya wouldn't cause trouble with Benjamin
right at hand, and she was still in a paranoiac
fog over Michael's identity. Benjamin naturally interpreted her hostile attitude as over-
protectiveness. Benjamin had hired Maggie's
husband, Philip. Perhaps Benjamin could prove
to be an ally . . . if someone could get the glint
of Tanya Walker out of his eyes so he could
see clearly.

Obediently, Tanya returned with a pair of
stiff blue clip-on owner ID tags. "Here are
your passes. Good-bye, Mr. Knight." She
walked away on Benjamin's arm in a hurry.

"Don't be so irate, love," Michael heard
Benjamin say to her as they walked away.
"You seem to think there's a thug or assassin
hiding under every flat rock. . . ."

Michael spotted Maggie near the grandstand,
looking around in the milling crowd for Buddy,
who had run off to inspect the contestants'
cars.

He held up an owner's pass between two
fingers. "Here you go; you may take your
rightful place among Silicon Valley's gentry."

"You're a doll," she said with genuine
pleasure. "Now if only I could find the heir to
my throne . . . Buddy? Buddy!"

"He'll turn up. It's a few minutes yet until
the green flag and there's lots of cars to gawk
at." He accompanied Maggie to her seat in
the section of the grandstand cordoned off
with blue ropes. Revving cars were beginning
to take their places at the start mark on the

broad oval track. "I think that's my cue," Michael said, and turned back toward the stairs.

"Hey!" Maggie jumped after him and left a light kiss on his cheek. "For luck."

"You just watch me show Com Tron a few tricks, lady." He ran back to his car, quickly strapping himself into the pilot bucket and firing up. The computerized dashboard came to life and the PURSUIT lightbar blinked insistently.

"Not yet, KITT," he said. "Keep your shirt on."

He slotted himself into the second string of cars between a supercharged Dodge and a ballistically contoured Chevy that looked much like his own car.

One of the video screens popped on, reading out AUXILIARY SHOULDER BELT and blinking.

A second belt dropped from the ceiling and Michael rapidly buckled it. Now his torso was crisscrossed with belts in the manner of the competing drivers. The screen obligingly went dark.

The engines sounded like a hundred angry, hungry jungle beasts. Noise was all around him. Michael keyed up the windows on both sides and the interference dwindled away to a background murmur. He grabbed the wheel, vision hopping from the waiting flag to the blinking blue PURSUIT bar. "Okay, Devon," he said to himself. "Let's find out if you're just another mad scientist, or if you know your stuff."

He depressed the PURSUIT bar.

The green flag in the hands of the starter whipped down while the grandstand loud-speaker blatted: "And the race is on!" The smoke and dust of takeoff rose all around Michael's car, and he put the accelerator full down. For perhaps the only time during the derby, the drivers fanned apart, giving each other room to jockey around and try their luck at demolishing each other.

Michael's car shot between two others and plowed hard into the first turn of the race. Suddenly the Chevy glided in from the right, intending to broadside Michael back into his former position. Michael cranked quickly left and took the steam out of the Chevy's blow. The two cars merely ground against each other, shuddering with impact. Then the Chevy veered outward to try strafing him again.

"Wow!" came Buddy's thrilled voice from the backseat. "This is *far out*!" He poked his head out between the seats.

Startled, Michael did not even have time to ask the boy what he was doing stowing away in the car, because the Chevy was coming for them a second time at over a hundred miles an hour.

7

From the sky, the Newtown Dirt Racing Center looked like a huge figure eight, and the twenty or more cars chewing up the track resembled ball bearings rattling around inside a tube: crashing, rebounding, cutting in front and behind each other, and barreling suicidally onward at increasing speed . . . just to go around in a circle one more time.

Instinctively, Michael fast-braked while Buddy's head was still between the seats. The boy's shoulders took the deceleration pressure without hurting him, and KITT's numeral speedometer noted the rapid drop from 98 mph to 30 as the rear end of the car vibrated heavily, slipping on the dirt surface. The track was not designed for panic stops, only endless forward motion. Clouds of billowing brown dust were already surrounding the cars and rising from the track.

As KITT nosed down with a gravel-dragging noise, the red Chevy that had already tried to boom them continued its sideswiping charge. But its driver had not reckoned with KITT's ability to dump speed without sliding and could not abort his trajectory once the crossing motion was begun.

The Chevy sliced across the track in front of KITT, hard into the elbow of the track's first turn, and kept going. The momentum that would have been absorbed by smashing sideways into Michael's car now took the Chevy careening into the inside guardrails. White wooden posts were clipped like toothpicks and shot upward from the nose of the Chevy in a spray, littering the track and drawing applause from the crowd in the grandstand.

Maggie's knuckles whitened on the rail in front of her. She suspected why Michael had slowed down rather than playing chicken with the Chevy, and why Buddy had not yet turned up.

"What do you think you're doing back there!" Michael yelled, more angry with himself for failing to notice his diminutive stowaway in the backseat than with Buddy for taking advantage of the opportunity in the first place.

Buddy watched with obvious pleasure as the Chevy wiped itself out on the guardrails, but when the car slowed and he turned to Michael it was with disappointment. "How come you didn't *ram* him? Why'd ya chicken out?"

"You're supposed to be with your mother!"

"Aw, give me a break . . . this is more fun!"

They were losing valuable seconds. Even KITT was impatient; the PURSUIT bar had started blinking again, urging Michael to get on with it.

"Okay, okay. Get your butt into the seat and strap yourself in. Hurry up!"

As Buddy scrambled between the seats another auxiliary shoulder harness dropped from the car's ceiling.

"Move it, Buddy!" Michael was pleased with the way his command speeded up Buddy's already excited movements. Adult authority had been reestablished.

From the bleachers, Maggie saw the black car begin to pick up speed, nudging outward from the crook of the first curve. The voice of the grandstand announcer made her throat tighten.

"Number Seven, the Chevy driven by Don Farrell, has already been eliminated! Tough luck, Don! See you next year! Meanwhile, the independent entry, Number Twelve, is spinning his wheels on the inside of—no, wait a minute! There he goes! He's not out of the race yet, ladies and gents! Now we'll see some real action—as the cars approach racing speed, the intersection of the figure eight will be pretty hairy. The trick in this race, folks, is to get through that intersection without wiping yourself out against the two-way flow. And there! Number Twelve is trying to make up for lost time by challenging the last car in the line, Number Fifteen, driven by Art Logan! Will he back down again? Logan is a two-time winner of this race and isn't likely to cut the new boy any slack. . . ."

Acceleration squashed Buddy back into his seat as Michael put KITT back into the PURSUIT mode and tried to regain lost ground. They were now hindmost in the race. But being first is not the only object of a demolition derby, Michael knew. There was also survival. That was why the car just ahead, Number Fifteen, was hugging the outside rail. He was waiting for the little fish in the race to bump themselves off so he could get down to the serious competition among the last five or so die-hards. He gave Michael token resistance, then let him zip ahead and into the slot. Number Fifteen promptly added some gas and tapped KITT's rear bumper to let Michael know he was now boxed in.

"Wise guy," muttered Michael. He veered KITT away and Number Fifteen cut to the right to avoid crashing, losing a lot of his paint on the right side against the outer rails.

The next opponent in KITT's sights was not so accommodating. Number Four, a lumbering canary-yellow fastback, cut across to prevent Michael from gaining any more distance. Michael would have to drop back or shoot into the guardrails.

He did neither.

He speeded up to within an inch of the fastback's rear bumper, then shot left as both cars screamed up on the outside of the next

turn. The driver of Number Four was too busy
trying to keep Michael from passing, and
undercompensated. He pulled hard to the left
to block Michael, and the next thing he saw
was the sharp curve of the guardrail in front
of him.

Michael cranked hard left, taking the turn.
The yellow fastback punched through the rails
and went airborne for a second. It would have
landed rough on four wheels if one of the
Com Tron service trucks had not been parked
outside the rail. A pit crew scattered when
they saw the car flying at them. With a metal-
rending screech, Number Four touched down
in the middle of the tractor-trailer's box. Auto
parts scattered in a hundred different directions and the truck teetered like a bowling
pin before it decided to lie down on its side
with a crash. The yellow fastback stood on its
nose for a precarious second, then somersaulted
forward, ripping the tin roof from the trailer
and flattening its own roof to the level of
the doors when it met the ground. Number
Four was out of the race.

"Hey, neat!" exclaimed Buddy. "You not
only wiped him out but you wiped out the
truck, too! Do it again!"

Michael looked at the kid, thinking, You
wanna drive, hotshot?—and decided not to
ask.

The spectacular crash apparently made the
announcer's whole day, and while he enthusiastically recounted the action, Will Benjamin
cast a dour eye on Tanya, seated beside him

in the owner's bleachers. "These boys aren't supposed to cost me any trucks, Tanya. Where'd you scare up the new drivers, skid row? I thought these were professionals!"

"They are," Tanya said, burning. She kept her eyes on the black auto that was causing most of the trouble so far.

Number Fifteen was still large in KITT's rearview mirrors, bumper hugging. Directly ahead, blocking Michael's further progress, were the glimmering rear decks of Number Nine and Number Twenty, bobbing and weaving for position. Dust sprayed up and covered the windshield; KITT's blowers deflected it just as quickly. Nine and Twenty shifted heavily, banging together and bouncing apart. There was a scant three feet or so between them. Michael was sandwiched, unable to pass, with Number Fifteen eating his tailpipe.

"We're in trou-bllle," Buddy said in a singsong tone of doom, delighted by this new impending disaster.

"KITT," said Michael. The panel voice monitor of the car responded, its red light fluctuating. "We need to knock out four feet or so ahead of us. I'm switching PURSUIT to the AUTO mode. You figure out what to do."

"*As you wish,*" said KITT. Was Michael mistaken, or was the car's answer . . . respectful?

The light pattern on the dash shifted itself, and KITT reduced the lag space between itself and the two lead cars to nothing. As the whole parade soared into another broad loop of the

figure-eight track, there was a brief, disorienting lurch of vertigo as the Knight Industries
2000 pushed off, balancing on its two left
wheels at 100 mph. The end-standing car easily fit into the narrow slot between Nine and
Twenty, its right-hand wheels rolling easily
along Twenty's roofline. Buddy yelped and
hung on. Michael saw the dirt track skim by
inches from the window on his side. In seconds they had negotiated the slot. The drivers
of the opposing cars were too stunned to do
anything but gape, and as soon as KITT passed
them they began to drift together. The driver
of Number Twenty, on the right, recovered
first, overcorrecting. His vehicle swung out of
the pattern and took out some more of the
outer guardrail. It crashlanded off center, its
hood shearing loose and flying backward over
the car. The impact snapped the front axle
and the wheels rolled away in different directions as Number Twenty slid to a halt against
one of the bales of hay installed around the
perimeter of the track. Oil smoke rolled up
from the undercarriage of the wreck. The
driver climbed out and gave his useless machine a savage kick.

Number Fifteen slid into the race position
vacated by Twenty and decided to eliminate
Number Nine just as Michael's car dropped
back to all fours with a resilient thump, not
losing a bit of speed. They were rolling up on
the intersection again, and with keen timing
Number Fifteen, Logan, forced Number Nine
to brake directly into the path of an oncom-

ing car from the other half of the track. Nine took the onrushing car full in the right side, and both cars spun out, parts and smoke floating everywhere.

"And Cars Number Nine and Five just bit the big one right in the center of the intersection!" the announcer screamed, beside himself. "What a race! There goes Romero, the driver of Number Nine. If I was him, I'd get outta the way of these lunatics, too! He had to dive for the island, there, but he appears to be okay. But it looks like Number Five's driver, Brad Standish, has a little bone to pick with Romero for zapping him out of the race like that! Standish just punched Romero in the face! Romero responds with an uppercut! A great takedown by Standish, and they're rolling in the dirt! A left by Romero! A flurry of rabbit punches by Standish, knocking the big Spanish mechanic back! Another powerhouse left! Standish is wobbling now . . . !"

The crowd was cheering wildly at Michael's wheel-standing stunt, the race in general, and the fistfight going on in the pits.

"Uh-oh, folks, it looks like Car Number Thirteen is in a little bit of a spot!

Michael saw the whole thing happen right in his path. Number Thirteen was a mean, low-slung Pontiac with fat racing mags that had zoomed too fast into the far turn and begun to spin the car like a dervish, throwing away a spiraling plume of dust. The driver could not regain control, and the torque from plowing along the track sideways levered off one of his front wheels. The exposed lug chomped into the ground and anchored the Pontiac to full stop just in time for its rear end to be smashed away by the car just ahead of Michael, Number One. Michael leaned on the wheel to no effect. KITT was still in the AUTO mode.

"KITT, return control to me now!" It was too late.

Buddy saw that Michael's hands were not on the wheel as KITT neatly evaded the wreckage of Number Thirteen, diverting around it as it had around the semi truck on the first night Michael had ever sat in the pilot's seat.

"Thanks, KITT," said Michael, grabbing the wheel. "I needed that."

"You're quite welcome, Michael. It's nice to be communicating again. . . ."

"Geez!" shouted Buddy, staring wide-eyed at the dash. "This thing even talks!"

Flustered, Michael said, "That's just the radio, Buddy. "Sometimes—"

"Hey! I may be just eight, but I'm not *dumb*," said Buddy. "This car just talked back to you. You said thank you and it said you were welcome."

Behind them, another car with less perfect timing center-punched the dead Pontiac and flew apart wildly.

"You're right, kiddo," Michael said. "But I think it might be a better idea if that was our little secret, okay?"

"I think I know what you mean." He stared

intently at the dash and said, "Hey, can it talk to me, too?"

Michael watched Number Fifteen, the car that had been riding his bumper, shoot past him on the inside of the next curve, marrying up ahead of him with Car Number One. "If you ask it a question," he said.

"Hey, car!" Buddy leaned against his shoulder harness, trying to put his nose closer to the dash. "Are we gonna win the race?"

"Go ahead, KITT, answer him," said Michael, amused.

"Young man," said KITT. *"Right now I am more urgently concerned with whether we shall* SURVIVE *this race. Mr. Knight possesses certain extraordinary skills as a driver, but on occasion these are overshadowed by his somewhat careless attitude with regard to"*—

"That's enough, KITT," Michael said, and Buddy laughed.

Ahead of them the two cars had slowed just a bit. Michael squinted; it seemed as though the two drivers were shouting at each other through their open windows.

"Number Thirteen is officially out of the race," the announcer's voice buzzed from the far end of the track. "And Number Thirteen wasn't so lucky for Number Three, either! Both cars are out! That leaves fourteen vehicles in operating condition . . . but not for long, ladies and gentlemen! There goes Number Nineteen!"

Across the track from Michael, Number Nineteen suddenly went end over end into the outside railings to a messy finish. The driver clambered out of the trash-compacted mess and got a round of applause from the crowd.

Michael watched Cars Fifteen and One, just ahead. What on earth were the drivers discussing at—he checked the red digital speedometer—at a 110 miles an hour?

"Hey, Carney!" shouted the driver of Number Fifteen.

"Hey, Logan!" Carney shouted back. He checked his rearview mirror; the black independent entry was still back there behind him. The jetwash of air made communication almost impossible.

"You see that hotshot's trick moves back there?"

"Yeah!"

"Michael, I've locked in on the exchange taking place between the drivers of the two cars just ahead. If you'll key in the audio speaker to your—"

"Which button!" Michael overrode KITT, frustrated. He looked down to see one of the toggles on the display just below the gearshift knob blinking, and he pushed up.

Amplified wind interference whooshed through the car, followed by Carney's voice: "... trying to horn in on prize money that rightfully belongs to either you or me! You catch my meaning?"

Michael saw the back of the head of Car Fifteen's driver bob in agreement as his voice came over the intercom speaker: "Loud and clear. Let's give this boy a little bit of room to get closer. Then we'll boom him."

The cars spread apart, and Michael began to inch up on the open space. "Those fellows are so generous," he said.

"But they're gonna squash you!" said Buddy.

KITT's voice came on, apprehensively, *"Michael, if I might suggest—"*

Michael noted the blinking light, one of the first buttons in KITT's repertoire he had ever pushed, and with surprising results. It had been included in Devon's too-short briefing. "The turbo boost." He nodded. "I was just thinking of that myself."

The black car slid between One and Fifteen until they were three abreast. "Come on, guys, let's get physical," Michael said, grinning at Carney and Logan through the side windows.

The flanking cars closed in like the jaws of a vise, locking KITT between them. The procedure was standard dirty play: to steer the victim into a catastrophe and split off at the last second. Michael saw they intended to run him through the inside wall on the upcoming turn.

Buddy covered his eyes. "Look out!"

Michael stabbed the white turbo boost buttons, and with a compression rush of several Gs KITT became airborne for a split instant, leap-frogging out of the grip of its two opponents and crunching to the ground *ahead* of them. The black car sped away.

Carney and Logan banged together when KITT slipped from between them, and both men fought to regain control of their vehicles. Up ahead, KITT cut neatly around the demolished remains of another entry— Number Sixteen—and Carney and Logan separated again, each dodging around one end of the wreck.

Cars One and Fifteen moved together for another conference, one KITT did not overhear.

"What the hell did you do?" screamed Carney, red-faced.

"I didn't go nothing, man! He just *flew* out from between us!" Logan watched the track action for a second as somebody else spun out and obliterated a bale of hay. The race was over for Number Two, another Com Tron truck driver named Dugan.

"Let's take him down!"

"Me first," yelled Logan. "Nobody makes a fool outta me!" His car jumped ahead of Carney's in pursuit of the black independent.

Michael's attention was on a tangle in traffic before him when Number Fifteen thudded heavily into his rear bumper. This was not like the scary coercion that had occurred previously; this was more like ramming. The two cars met again with a crunch.

"He can't do that!" said Buddy, craning his neck to look backward. "It's against NASCAR regulations!"

Again they were nudged heavily forward by the impact—*wham*!

"Somehow," said Michael, "I don't think this is a regulation race, Bud, old boy." *Wham!*

Buddy's attention turned to the transmission-hump console. Twenty pushbuttons glittered at him, and his hand reached out to browse through them.

Michael tore his concentration away from the track again. "Hey, don't start poking things at random. I'm not even sure what some of those do, yet."

"Yeah, but the last one made us fly!" Buddy protested.

They were struck again from behind. *Wham!* Then Logan, in Number Fifteen, dropped back a car length or so to build up more destructive ramming speed.

With the unswervable conviction children use to guide their actions even in the face of possible adult retribution, Buddy depressed what was to him the most prominent button. It made the characteristic touch-tone sound and went dark. Nothing happened.

"Hey! Hands off!" Michael's hand drew back to slap Buddy's away.

To the immediate left of the rear license plate, a thin moly-aluminum nozzle unsheathed itself, protruding far enough out from KITT to avoid getting any of its spray on the car itself. Then it cut loose with a thick cascade of viscous black oil, spattering Number Fifteen's front grille and windshield with impenetrable ooze.

Logan cursed and laid on the brakes—too late. His radials struggled for traction atop the frictionless oil slick. Car Fifteen began to spin out.

The audience oohed and aahed as Number

Fifteen flashed around and around, first losing a hubcap, then a wheel, then the trunk cover. Parts flew out from the eye of the miniature hurricane of circular motion, and the car continued spinning while mechanics leapt out of its twisting path. It finally smacked an infield speaker pole and stopped. Logan's part in the competition was finished.

Having completed its fifteen-second burst, the nozzle retracted and closed up.

"Wow! Just like James Bond!" Buddy was ecstatic.

Behind them and gaining, Carney, in Car Number One, was not so thrilled. He ducked around the oily patch on the field and pushed himself closer to Michael's car.

"Buddy, keep your hands *off* the console!" Michael swerved to avoid another smoldering former contestant.

"But I saved us, didn't I?"

"Yes—just don't touch anything else, okay?"

"But that other dirty rat who tried to make us crash is coming! Lemme push one more— just one, please?"

"Forget it! Sit tight. I'll take care of him. I'm not going to let this car do everything for me!"

Buddy appeared to calm down, but his eyes were hungrily scanning the remaining buttons. His vision locked on to one in particular.

SMOKESCREEN. It blinked once or twice.

Inside his car, Carney was talking to himself to build up his anger: "Okay, pal—you're up against Numero Uno now, and heaven help you."

Buddy monitored Michael warily, waiting for just the right moment to sneak a poke at the blinking button. Car Number One was moving up fast behind them and to the right.

On the other side of the KNIGHT license plate, a tiny hatch popped open. Dense white smoke spumed forth, kicking up a whirling fog bank in the wake of Michael's car.

Carney sped right into the middle of the earthbound cloud and lost his bearings. He tried manfully to stay on course by following the curve of the track, but had to give it up. There wasn't a foot of visibility to use.

"Damn!" Carney was in the grip of growing panic. Any second now he'd—

"Ladies and gentlemen," the announcer's voice echoed from the speakers, "it looks like the maverick in Car Number Twelve has finally run out of luck! It appears he's blown out his engine!"

Maggie stood up from her seat and shouted into the race-track noise. Nobody heard her.

Michael heeled over into the next turn, and in his mirrors saw Carney shoot out of the cloud cover, still aimed dead straight. Carney saw the railing coming at him, but if he turned at this late date it would only be to smash into another part of the restricting fence.

Number One tore away nine feet of fencing as it kicked through and rolled in the air, setting down in a power skid that tipped it over onto its right side and slid it another fifty feet before running out of energy. It almost cleared an old mobile-home–style concession stand set up well away from the track.

"And it's bye-bye time for Number One, driven by Arthur Carney, folks. And Number Twelve is about to get the black flag, disqualifying it from the race due to the engine trouble it seems unable to shake . . . no, wait just a minute!"

Inside the car, Michael was admonishing Buddy again to unhand the control console. When Buddy removed his finger from the button the smoke flow instantly stopped.

"An amazing turn of events, folks!" said the announcer. "Car Number Twelve is actually picking up speed, and—" He was distracted by a horrific, grating crash as two other cars met head-on at the intersection of the figure eight. "But I can't say Cars Ten and Eighteen were so lucky!"

Out on the field the junked cars slowed down and fell apart with shocking totality— some of these Detroit monsters were not put together very well and tended to disassemble in ways guaranteed to make the fans a bit self-conscious when they got into their own cars to drive—carefully—home.

Out on the field the flag man quickly tossed away the black disqualification flag he had drawn out for Michael and picked up the checkered flag. Six cars were still in the running, and it was nearly finish time.

Michael was making up for lost time and gaining on the apparent winner, Number

Seventeen, who breezed through the intersection ahead of him. Unless he cut speed, KITT was going to obliterate Number Eleven, headed right for him from another arm of the figure eight. And if he cut speed, it seemed certain he would lose the race.

Just as the two were about to hit—Eleven did not slow down because its driver, a man named Dolan, wanted to win just as badly—Michael punched the turbo boost button.

KITT vaulted into midair like a car coming over the top of a San Francisco hill. Its wheels cleared the roof of Number Eleven by a good four feet and hit the ground spinning. Michael and Number Seventeen slewed into the last turn, Michael sticking close to the inside and gaining the advantage. When the checkered flag flashed down, he was three car lengths ahead.

"Hey Buddy," said Michael. "We won."

Buddy looked out from behind the hands that had flown to his eyes when KITT jumped into the air. "We *won*?"

In the distance, Michael could see Maggie jumping up and down like a cheerleader. The announcer was babbling about how he still could not believe what he had just seen.

Michael pulled to the inside of the track and got out. The figure eight was a junkyard of mangled automobiles, all leaking and steaming viciously.

Over near Maggie was someone surveying the aftermath of the race through field glasses. Michael spotted Tanya Walker's black leather

getup and knew it had to be Will Benjamin
watching . . . which was just the way he preferred events to be.

"From here it doesn't look like the black
car has a mark on it," Benjamin, incredulous,
said to Tanya. "That automobile is incredible.
You say that young man contacted you first,
earlier? Well, now I want you to make a point
of contacting him. I want all his statistics,
and everything you can find out about that
car!" He tilted the binoculars away from his
face and confronted Tanya directly. "I want
to know where he comes from, and where
that car comes from!"

Tanya's expression toward the car on the
track, and the man getting out of it, was
venomous. "That makes two of us," she said,
looking around for Fred Wilson, her comrade
from the Consolidated Chemical Corporation
job. To Benjamin she said, "I'll get right on
it. Darling."

8

As soon as Maggie saw Buddy climb from the passenger side of the black car, she jumped easily over the rail in front of the owner's bleachers and ran across the field to him. Michael watched her. She made pretty admirable time. He turned from admiring her running form and continued on his own way across the track toward Tanya's position.

She stood her ground defiantly, arms folded. Benjamin had escaped temporarily, citing some mundane errand as excuse. To Michael she seemed overpoweringly sure of herself, a domineering animal, attractive and very deadly, like a poisonous flower. Her blood-red scarf drifted on the light wind like the muffler of a biplane pilot.

"So. The winner arrives," she said with a slight smirk.

"You asked before what I was selling," said Michael evenly. "You just saw it. Interested?"

"I'm interested in the car *and* the driver," she said. She had not budged from her pose.

Michael thought that anybody who could lie as convincingly and sweetly as Tanya did regularly would have no trouble taking over the top positions of string-pulling power inside a corporate octopus like Com Tron. He had to force himself to remember that this was the woman who had *murdered* him. It was true: Michael Long had died, but Michael Knight had been born of his ashes. In an alien and peculiar way, Tanya was to be thanked for what she had done. At the same time, the ghosts of Michael Long and Wilton Knight needed avenging. God only knew how many of Tanya's other past victims were lined up behind those two. The blizzard of orange fire and the solid wall of agony that had accompanied the bullet she shot into his face played back in his brain insistently. He could reach out to her right now and break her neck within seconds. But that would only be lopping off one of the hydra heads of her espionage network. Two new heads would replace it. If he could apprehend her and her crew with some rock-hard, red-hot evidence, he could kill the entire beast.

"I'm prepared to tell you a little more about the car and discuss terms," Michael finally said with a smile. "But not here. I want you—or whomever you represent if you're not big enough—to meet me tonight at the House of the Rising Sun. Eight o'clock sharp or no news is bad news for you."

Tanya, who would naturally consider no one else to be more important than herself, would show up, he felt sure. Her own ego would force her to rise to his bait. "Why at that place?" She looked as though she wanted him to admit the reason had something to do with dragging her into one of the rooms the bar rented.

"I'm not a local boy, and it's the only place I'm familiar with around here. What's the matter? Too plebeian for your taste?"

Her features grew stony. "I'll be there. You just make sure you are, too."

Michael wheeled and walked back to his car.

Tanya quickly made her way back to the credentials booth, where she found Fred Wilson waiting for her. The husky operative was clad in a close-fitting gray version of his habitually affected three-piece "power suit." Only a slight bulge at the left armpit betrayed the presence of an enormous .44 Magnum—the portable cannon of a handgun made popular by the movies. He lounged against one of the booth's posts.

"Great race," he said in a voice edged with sarcasm.

Tanya was all business. "What have you got on him?"

"Michael Knight does not exist," he said clinically. "That is, up until three months ago."

She regarded him. They both knew that three months ago—give or take a few weeks— they had been running the scam against Consolidated Chemical in Las Vegas. "Fake identity?"

"His documents—driver's license, credit cards—all originate in the same *week*. All brand new. No doubt about it that it's a phony identity . . . or a cover that doesn't run very deep."

"If that car is some kind of industrial prototype, then the fake ID doesn't surprise me. He seems to be in the same racket we are. Different branch. He wants to negotiate for that car we all just saw."

Wilson grew agitated. "Since when do we put out want ads saying we're in the market for anything? Ours isn't the type of business to go public, Tanya!"

"I didn't say yea or nay to him," she lied, to avoid an argument.

He would not let it go. "It's one thing to rip off secrets from a development lab and sell them to the highest bidder or the fattest competitor. It's quite another to stroll away with a prototype I'm sure the whole company is paying vast sums to search out, assuming it's stolen. What if it's military, Tanya? Do you want army intelligence breathing down *your* neck?" He huffed and straightened his cuffs. "I say this whole situation screams 'setup.' "

"Did you run his fingerprints?" It was an unnecessary question. Wilson was thorough.

"First thing. I don't have them, the cops don't have them, and the government computers don't have them. Some people still believe prints are only on file if the subject has a criminal record. We know better. But Michael Knight—or whatever his name really is—isn't in anyone's file or data bank.''

''What about law enforcement? Any way to trace that?''

''We'd need to pull our own set of his prints to compare.''

''And Fred,'' she said with a knowing grin. ''Can you possibly think of any way we might get ourselves a set of his fingerprints?'' She was playing the smug female, leaving the matter—and the dirty work—entirely in his hands.

Wilson nodded, assessing mentally just what would be required. He looked out over the race track at all the ruined automobiles, still smoking and groaning. ''Yeah,'' he said. ''I can think of one way that might work.''

The ride back to Maggie's duplex was a near-constant flood of talk, with everybody going full steam at the same time. It was Buddy, however, who did the most talking, detailing each facet of the demolition derby to his mom with hysterical excitement. Michael laughed with pleasure. And KITT wisely stayed silent, a third partner to the secret shared with Michael and Buddy, who would never tell until it was irrelevant anyway.

''Luce's off today,'' said Maggie, tucking one leg beneath the other on the car seat. ''It's just me and Buddy the Kid.'' She hesitated, then said, ''I never was a good cook, you know? TV dinners only, and a lot of stuff out of plastic cartons. But Luce taught me one thing, one saving grace."

"And what might that be?" said Michael, smelling food in the offing.

"How to make the meanest enchiladas you'll find in all of northern California. Now if you know the state well at all, you know that there isn't a decent Mexican restaurant north of Los Angeles, except for a few renegade LA-style places that happen to be in San Francisco. Which means you're invited for dinner. Say no and I'll be emotionally crushed because it's the only standard domestic skill I really have."

"Yeah!" prompted Buddy. "Mom makes *terrific* enchiladas!"

"Buddy usually eats over half what I make, so I'll have to make twice as much, I suppose—"

"I love good enchiladas, Maggie, but I've—"

She waved her hand and narrowed her eyes. "It looks like you're getting ready to say no. There's always a sentence with a *but* in it. 'Sure, you look terrific, Maggie, *but.*' 'Sure you make great enchiladas, Maggie, *but.*' *But* is going to be inscribed on my tombstone, I just know it."

"Listen, Maggie," said Michael. "I'm positive the enchiladas will be superior, and I already know the company is charming. Grant me a rain check. I've got to go back to the House of . . . you know, that place where you started the Friday night beer-bath tradition."

The humor dropped from her tone. "Business or pleasure?"

"Business. Tonight. Pleasure would be you and the enchiladas."

"It's Tanya Walker again, isn't it?"

"I threw out the bait this afternoon. Now I've got to see if I can catch anything."

"You mean the stunts you did with the car?"

"Mm-hm. Just the thing Tanya and her coterie of spies would salivate over."

"Michael, this is starting to sound a little creepy . . . you're beginning to talk like—" She broke off suddenly, holding her tongue. They had arrived at the duplex.

Buddy was shoving his way out of the backseat of the car almost before it had stopped.

"Buddy!" Maggie commanded sharply. "Get back here this instant and tell Mr. Knight that—"

"I know, I *know*," said Buddy. "I gotta say thank you." He did a flamboyant little bow. "Thanks, Mr. Knight. Thank you, thank you, thank you—I gotta go tell *everybody* what happened!" He dashed off to find some of his neighborhood buddies.

"He's a good kid," said Michael.

"A real prince, when he's not hiding out in strange cars. He might have gotten hurt, you know, and then where would we all be?"

"Trust me, Maggie, it's nearly impossible for him to get hurt in this car—for the same reasons that made some of my stunt moves out there today possible. And I made sure he was strapped in."

"I know," she said. "I saw you slow down for no reason. I think that's when I guessed what had happened. If it had been just you in the car, you wouldn't have stopped for safety's sake."

"When I'm on my own I tend toward reck-lessness." He remembered what KITT had said earlier. "Some of my best friends say it's my most annoying trait."

"Well," she said, fidgeting. "That's what I was about to say when I remembered Buddy was still in the car. That the way you talk about nailing Tanya and Com Tron, you sound the same way my husband did before he took them on and got ... had his accident ... I mean, got *killed* for his trouble. I can never say it: *got killed.* For all I know Tanya gave the order to murder him herself. Maybe she even participated. Philip *got killed* doing ex-actly what you want to run off and do now. And here I am offering you dinner and talk and almost ... hell, *anything* else, if you'll just stay away from those people. You can't beat them; one man or one woman can't do anything against them. They're unbeatable, so it's best to let the wounds heal as they can and just try not to let them screw up your life any more." Her eyes had grown shiny. "I felt so good when you won today. Like I'd won against them, too."

"I had a benefactor who firmly believed that one person *could* make a difference," said

Michael. "That's why I have to go do this, Maggie. I'll be back for dinner, I promise." He dug out a tissue for her. "And don't cry . . . I thought you said you had a great day."

"I did," she said, pausing to blow her nose. Then she looked at him, deeply. "Who are you? Who are you really?"

He placed his free hand over hers. "A friend, Maggie. Really."

"Do you know what you're up against?" she said.

"We've been through all that. Com Tron is just—"

"I'm not talking about Com Tron," she said, cutting him off. "I'm talking about *me*. I'm talking about the way I hurt after the *last* man who made me feel . . ." She started again. "You know the big emotional disaster everybody has in their life? The one that crushes your spirit and makes you bitter? Well, I've had mine several times over. I think there must be two or three people walking the earth without their own disasters because I got them, too. I don't want to go through all that again."

Then she surprised Michael by grabbing the back of his neck in her hand and pulling him forward into a long-lasting kiss. When they broke apart she fled the car, still clutching her tissue.

"I can't make heads or tails out of what you two were just talking about," said KITT as Michael stared after Maggie. *"Can you explain it to me, Michael?"*

"There was a lot of telepathy involved,"

said Michael. "A lot of communication having nothing to do with spoken words or significant motions."

"It seems that you and the young lady share a number of identical experiences, if there is no need for you to specify."

"That's a good way to put it, KITT."

The House of the Rising Sun seemed to be doing payday business in the wake of the race at the Newton track. Cars and trucks filled the front and back parking lots, spilling over into the capacious after-hours slots to be had in the parking lot of the savings and loan complex next door. Michael caught a couple pulling out and appropriated their spot, pulling the black Knight Industries 2000 into the just-vacated space. He could already hear the music coming from the bar.

"Michael, logic would seem to dictate that another excursion into that establishment is likely to produce results much like those of your first visit, only intensified. Are you sure this is a prudent course of action?"

Michael got out of the car. "I'll never be able to say you didn't tell me so, KITT. Let's see if I can trap Tanya Walker . . . for a change." He closed his door before KITT had another chance to protest in his superior, almost snobbily academic fashion. Funny, thought Michael, I've started thinking of the car as a *him* instead of an *it*. Hadn't some psychologist warned that anthropomorphizing one's automobile was an unhealthy symptom reflecting a need for human contact when none was available?

He decided to make his entrance via the front way, and walked around. If Tanya was waiting inside, she would have arranged herself so as to be in the most strategic position— probably he'd have to walk through a gaggle of Com Tron goons to get to the booth where she held court.

Michael pushed open the door and walked in.

He got the distinct feeling that he was the young gunslinger entering the hostile saloon in history's most clichéd western scenario. Seated at the bar and slouched in a few of the booths were enough surly types to populate a post office's ten-most-wanted bulletin board, and they all looked up and ceased talking as the door shut behind Michael. They placed half-drained mugs pointedly back on the tables and seemed to stiffen in anticipation. All the other customers for the night in the House of the Rising Sun must have been upstairs in the other lounge area, or on the dance floor. In the central room with the big bar it was just Michael, a Mongol horde in trucker vests and grimy ball caps . . . and no sign of Tanya Walker.

He recognized them now. Seated at the bar nearest to the door was Logan, the driver in the demolition derby who had received a faceful of KITT's oil slick. Next to him was the driver whose yellow Mustang Michael and KITT had helped make part of a Com Tron service truck.

Other dim faces resolved themselves and became familiar. All of them had been drivers in the race that afternoon. Dolan, the swarthy pilot of Number Eleven—who would have rammed Michael full-on if Michael had not been able to turbo-boost over his rooftop—unhorsed himself from his stool and faced Michael.

"Hi fellas," Michael said with forced jocularity. "Uh—nice race."

"Why don't you and I talk about it outside?" said Dolan. His bunching fists indicated that a reminiscing conversation was the last thing on his mind.

Somebody else got to his feet and approached as Michael said, "Sorry, friend. I'm here to meet a young lady. You know Tanya Walker, right? She probably pays your salary, or pulls your strings. So we wouldn't want anything untoward to happen to me, since she requested I come here. Right?"

The oncoming figure emerged into a pool of light. "Miss Walker understood your message. She sent us down here to pick you up." It was Carney. Number One. The smokescreen had done him in earlier, and right now he did not look too jolly.

"You work for Tanya, too?" said Michael.

From the bar a man named Red clarified: "Her suggestion was that we show you just what we think of outsiders rolling into Millston, and distrupting our nice little local race,

and stealing prize money that rightfully belongs in the pockets of me and the boys, here."
Red was the man Michael had passed at the
last instant in order to win the race—Car
Number Seventeen.

"Hold it a second, then, would you?" said
Michael, holding up his hands but not backing off. "In that case I'm sure Tanya told you
that I plan to donate that money to charity.
Didn't she tell you?"

Carney grinned, cocking back his hat. "Yeah.
Well, we've each got a little donation for you,
too, Mr. Knight."

Michael walked casually over to the bar,
where Dolan had abandoned his mug of beer.
His eyes connected with those of George, the
barman with the pencil-thin mustache. George
hurriedly put down the highball glass he had
been polishing and fled the room. In the broad
back-bar mirror Michael saw the other drivers rise from their seats to converge on him.

"Fellas, I hate to have to mention this, but
I'm kind of heavily into martial arts." He
turned, elbows against the bar, and looked at
Dolan particularly. "You know?"

Several of the men laughed.

Dolan made a come-on gesture. "That Ori-
ental crap, huh? Big deal."

Michael saw Dolan's eyes tense, a sure sign
he was preparing to swing a haymaker blow
at Michael's head. Before Dolan could get his
ham-sized fist fully closed and airborne, Michael swept Dolan's mug from the bar and
dashed the beer in the man's face. When Dolan

shut his eyes for that split second, Michael broke the solid glass mug over his skull and the driver went down without even a grunt.

Then Michael's hands snapped back to the bar edge and he hoisted himself into the air, planting a boot heel into each of two more charging faces. They pinwheeled backward, missions aborted. Carney sank a pistonlike blow into Michael's stomach, doubling him over, and joined his fists for the overhead swing that would put the stranger into dreamland.

Michael pushed off from the floor and cleared Carney's legs from beneath him with a flat-handed lateral chop. Carney began to sit up and Michael gave him a fast elbow in the throat. Carney gagged and sat down hard.

Logan was coming for him with an up-raised whiskey bottle. Other men were shouting and shoving now, eager to join in the violent action. With a scissors motion of his hands Michael sent the bottle cartwheeling away to shatter on the floor. He rabbit-punched Logan several quick times but it was like hitting the jaw of a statue. Logan grabbed Michael's shirt-front and the silver oval of his belt buckle and hoisted him off the ground, to send him sprawling where he could be polished off.

When Michael hit the stone floor he rolled and came up relatively unbruised. He knew the first rule of fighting was *knowing how to fall down*—because if one did not know this, one might not ever stand up again. He put his

fists into a boxer's pose when Logan stomped
toward him, and this action threw off the
larger man's guard. Expecting more ineffectual punching and counting on absorbing
Michael's comparatively feeble blows in order to impress his buddies in the bar, Logan
was totally unprepared for the wheel kick that
jerked his head around as though magnetized.
Two of his front teeth landed on the other
side of the room and Logan became acquainted
with unconsciousness very quickly.

Someone put a full nelson on Michael from
behind, pinioning his arms down. Another goon
strode forward to perform a bit of facial rear-
rangement on Michael, several sharp-edged
turquoise signet rings adorning the fingers of
his meaty fist. Michael decided he liked his
new face the way it was and shot his arms
straight up, slithering free of the wrestling
hold and disabling the beringed man with a
well-placed puncture kick.

Michael whirled and confronted Red, who
had grabbed and rushed him; he butted Red
in the stomach with his head and railroaded
him backward to crash into a booth and scat-
ter beer mugs and peanut husks everywhere.
The booth table folded up under their combined weight, and Michael slapped Red's head
against the formica for good measure, to ensure that he wouldn't be such a nuisance.

He stood and turned around into a blow
that closed up his eyes and scattered white
lighting across the insides of his eyelids. He

caught a booth rail for support and blocked
the next punch, cupping his hand and batting his attacker's right ear. The man's face
scrunched up with pain when his eardrum
popped, and when Michael planted his fist
into that face it seemed to explode around his
hand. Another antagonist down, he thought.

But there were too many more to keep putting away like lemmings. Both the front door
of the bar and the access hallways were clot-
ted with people anxiously watching the fight,
cheering as they had at the demolition derby.
Michael even caught a fast glimpse of bet
money changing hands and spotted two of
the drivers beating each other up. He had no
way of knowing these two were Number Five
and Number Nine—Standish and Romero, the
same two who had been fighting on the track
earlier. But there were at least seven other
burly drivers hungry to pummel Michael into
mush, and as he shook the dizzy shock blur
from his vision they came for him. He deflected a fist and ducked quickly around an
open-handed grab, intending to put the bar
between himself and his attackers.

Someone—Farrell, Number Seven—latched
on to his legs as he dived for the bar, and
both men went knees-up into the bar mirror.
Somehow Michael suspected it would get
broken. Splinters of sharp, silvered glass pep-
pered them; demolished liquor bottles from
the mirror shelf emitted a dozen pungent
aromas. Farrell and Michael were inundated

in booze and broken glass. Farrell pushed up to hands and knees, getting both embedded with glass shards. He didn't have time to yell in pain before Michael socked him squarely on top of the head. Farrell went prone and silent.

Number Two, Dugan, was clambering over the bar to try his luck when a woman's voice made him hesitate.

"Hey! Dugan! No! Stop!"

Michael first thought, How nice, Maggie's come to save me. He sucked in a grateful breath, then thought: No, it's got to be Tanya. Only she could call off the dogs that way.

But it was neither. A face poked over the bar and he recognized it as that of Lonnie, who had spoken to him the first time he was in the House of the Rising Sun. He heard footsteps rush around the bar, heard expensive heels crunching the glass fragments to powder. When he looked up he saw the statuesque brunette leaning down over him. He wiped his face and felt blood dribbling from his mouth and nose.

"Oh my god, Mr. Knight, are you okay?" She briefly held his head in her hands, then moved behind him to help him up.

"No, Lonnie, but that doesn't—" That was all he said because as soon as he started to get to his feet, Lonnie, now behind him, brought a full Johnny Walker Red bottle down on the top of his head.

Glass nested in his hair and whisky flooded down around his face. The last thing Michael thought was, When vinegar doesn't work try sugar. Then he passed out on the floor at Lonnie's feet.

9

"You're *where*?"

Devon Miles was alone inside Wilton Knight's cavernous office on the Knight estate, and so he felt he could indulge his outrage by yelling. If the servants heard, they would respectfully ignore the outburst.

Michael Knight's voice crackled over the long-distance line. It was a bad connection; cross-talk from other conversations was impinging on his call. Two women were discussing the funeral of one's grandmother, and a reedy male voice was complaining about a past-due bill. These competing calls phased in and out of Michael's call, but there was something else distorting his message as well, Devon noticed. Michael's voice seemed slurred, as though his mouth was stuffed with cotton batting, or he was speaking through a handkerchief.

"I'm canned inside the jail at the Millston's sheriff's office, Devon. But I swear it's a—"

"A frameup, a trumped-up charge, a falsification," said Devon sternly. "Yes. It always is."

"Look," said Michael, obviously lowering his voice and cupping the receiver. Somebody in authority was probably watchdogging him nearby. But Devon doubted whether the line was free of uninvited listeners. Michael went ahead regardless: "The people we want are running this whole damned town! Working here is like being inside a medieval fortress."

Devon maintained his calm. "Michael, where is the Knight Two Thousand."

Long pause. "I'm not certain."

Devon punched a phone patch button on the desk console, and within seconds a digital display screen printed out the number from which Michael was calling. There was no need to triangulate; Michael was indeed locked up in the sheriff's office, according to the information in the computer. His finger hovered over a button on the fast-dial board that was coded simply: KITT.

Acidly, Devon said, "You mean to tell me that you've . . . *misplaced* it?"

"The cops impounded it. That wouldn't be so bad, normally. It would just sit in the impound yard until I posted bail. But they're being real nebulous about the charges, and they're exercising their so-called right to hold me for twenty-four hours before settling on the charges. Also, I think someone at Com

Tron—you know who I mean—sweet-talked the sheriff into letting the analysts at the corporation check the car out. It's probably inside the plant as we speak."

"Congratulations. You've managed to fulfill my every original expectation of you."

"Devon, we can fight later; what do we do right now?"

"Oh, wonderful," said Devon. "Now it's 'we.' When you roared out of here awhile back, practically over my foot, it was 'I.' "

"The guard's coming. I don't have any more time."

"Don't worry, Michael. I can be there personally in a few hours. In the meantime, I—we—have recourse to other means of immediate action."

"What do you mean other means? We have to—" The line peeped and went dead as the connection was broken.

Devon was startled by the abrupt hangup, but knew it was not Michael's doing. He depressed the cradle buttons and waited for the dial tone before hitting the button marked KITT.

There was the crackle of the special-frequency radio connection going through. A red bubble light on the phone console indicated the absence of surveillance on the call. A midrange beep sounded after which Devon enunciated very clearly: "Identification: Devon Miles. Code phrase for voice-print identification: 'How sharper than a serpent's tooth to have a thankless child.' "

KITT's synthetic voice sounded over the phone's monitor speaker. *"Hello, Mr. Miles. I'm afraid Mr. Knight may be in jeopardy."*

Devon cleared his throat and began to ask questions. In five minutes he knew what he needed to know.

Locally, the sheriff's office and the highway patrol shared the same office facilities, and Michael's jailer was none other than Deke Bannerman, the overweight country cop who had pulled him over on the way into Millston, near the famed necking hangout of Dead Man's Curve.

He clearly begrudged Michael his one phone call to the outside world, but whatever vestige of professional integrity remained in his soul forced him to allow it. Not that it mattered; in strict terms Michael had every constitutional right to plan on filing a lawsuit. But Deke and his buddies, like the truck drivers, like nearly everybody else in Millston, were working for Com Tron, not the government. When Com Tron was pleased, then he could go to work on plain, simple law and order.

So when he had figured the young stranger had logged enough time on the pay phone, he kicked his feet from where they were propped on the steel army-surplus office desk, walked across the room and put his sausagelike thumb down on the cradle tab. Once the prisoner was back in his cell, Deke could return to his coffee and men's magazine.

"Hey!" said Michael as he was cut off. "I wasn't finished! You'd better let me have another phone call!"

Deke laid his billy club alongside Michael's Adam's apple. That always shut them up, he thought. "I'll tell you this once, *boy*," He said. "It's time for you to go back to your suite. And keep quiet. You want trouble, you get a bullet in the leg and a charge of assaulting a peace officer. Now so far you've just got misdemeanor charges against you. Don't complicate my life *and* yours. Let's head on back to the cell."

Michael went peacefully. As they came through the access door to the cell block he asked, "What charges?"

Deke blew out a hefty breath. "Oh ... vandalism, disturbing the peace, brawling, public drunkeness. You'll probably get out in two days."

The open-cage cell door crashed shut and locked. "What about my rights?" said Michael.

"Boy," said Deke, turning back from the door. "In here you only got the rights *I* want to give you. You catch?"

Michael did not bother to acknowledge. Until Devon could pull a rabbit out of his hat, he would have to sit and wait. Deke returned to his office.

"Ole Deke the Geek," said a voice from the adjacent cell. One of the drivers, Carney, came into the light and wrapped his fingers around the bars. Michael ignored him and lay down on the steel bunk bolted to the opposite side of the cell. It was designed to hold a ratty mattress but had none. There was just a steel frame, flat as an operating table, painted industrial gray, and a moth-eaten square of army blanket—four feet on a side, not counting the holes. Michael stuffed it under his head, as a pillow.

"Hey. Hey, cowboy." Carney was still there.

Michael rolled over. It was no good.

"I'm talkin' to you, cowboy. I want to know what that machine of yours is made out of. There wasn't a nick on it after the race. What's the gimmick?"

"Sit and spin," growled Michael.

"Yeah, you're real tough, cowboy. You've impressed the hell out of everybody. You made Tanya take notice of you. You must be stupider than you look."

After a while Carney gave up and went back to his own business on the other side of his cell.

Tanya watched Michael Knight's jet-black wonder car being towed through the Com Tron gates. Standing beside her was Fred Wilson.

"Tell Symes to take the car over to the number-two shop and let the engineers take a few cracks at it."

"What do you mean?" said Wilson.

She looked him over and decided he was not a dunce after all. "I want to know where the parts for that automobile were fabricated. I want them to go over it with a microscope. Top to bottom, inside and out. Even specially customized or modified cars use stock parts, and the stock parts have serial numbers. We should be able to figure out where the work was done, and by whom." She moved off the catwalk balcony and into the corridor leading to Will Benjamin's suite of offices. "As for you, I want you to run Michael Knight's prints and get back to me with a report on those *and* on the car within the half hour."

Orders dispensed, she strode away. Wilson watched her for a moment.

Their relationship as hi-tech highwaymen had begun in the government furor over theft of computer secrets in the late 1970s and had been founded upon the unspoken agreement that both of them were on a more-or-less equal footing when it came to job selection and procedure. Wilson had infiltrated Consolidated Chemical and done most of the inside work on that job while Tanya took it easy playing Mata Hari—proffering herself as a bauble for Charles Acton, a shining toy bright enough to distract his notice from the covert pilferage taking place right in front of him. The Consolidated Chemical ripoff had been Fred Wilson's baby. With Com Tron, Tanya was doing the setups and Wilson was mostly hanging around waiting for something to do—such as processing the command he'd just received. He did not care for the tone Tanya used when she got into her commanding-general mode.

Their spy pool numbered about ten. Wilson picked certain operatives for efficiency or ruthlessness—such as Gray, the emotionless assassin who had smiled as he put a wadcutter into Muntzy's stomach in Las Vegas—or for specialty in certain technical fields such as computer accessing. Tanya had hand-selected female operatives such as Lonnie and Sally with a special eye toward a useful combination of allure and elementary espionage skills. Wilson often found himself looking over Tanya's corral of coral snakes; they almost frightened him. Fred Wilson secretly feared most women for the power they exerted over men who had made their fortunes crushing lesser men—men like Charles Acton, Will Benjamin and Wilton Knight.

The Knight job had been a dilly. That one had actually required Tanya to sweat a little, since the patriarch of Knight Industries had proven to be impervious to her spider's charms. Tanya had been compelled to do some extreme footwork to coordinate the theft of airplane design patents from the Knight computer banks. On that job she'd worked with a group of computer whizzes. She hated dependence on other people for the success of individual jobs, Wilson knew, but in order to climb her kind of ladder there would always have to be people to act as rungs. She was independent in spirit, but only as free as a vampire would be—always dependent on the exploitability of others. He wondered if she or any of her group had ever experienced an honest emotional attachment to another human being. Fred Wilson knew that *he* never had.

But Tanya was getting a bit power mad of

late. Her propensity for barking orders and expecting them to be carried out was becoming overbearing. True, she was the prime mover in this, the Com Tron job, but Wilson had noticed her trend toward a kind of totalitarianism over a period of months. Perhaps it would soon be time to cut her loose . . . before she disposed of him.

As soon as the Com Tron job was in the can, it might not be such a bad idea to aim Gray at Tanya and unleash him. Gray was a pretty peculiar human specimen himself, but of a kind Wilson had no trouble dealing with. Gray was honestly devoid of human feelings, too, but faithful as an attack dog. What he lacked in human attachments he compensated for with an unnatural savvy about machines. Wilson used Gray mostly as a hazard driver and airplane and chopper pilot. Gray's relationships were with the wheel of a car, the joystick of an aircraft or the trigger of his enormous Magnum artillery piece. It might not be such a bad idea to whip the Com Tron specifications out from under Tanya's nose, steal the super car they had just towed through the gates and put Gray behind the wheel of it when it was time to make the getaway. And, of course, dispose of Tanya.

Wilson's talents were in the area of informational access and infiltration. His instructions to the Com Tron drivers and to Deke Bannerman, the sheriff, had been merely to ensure that Michael Knight got arrested in order that his prints could be taken officially, not surreptitiously. Police-record prints were reliable and permanent, and required no sneaking around, no midnight dusting of the mystery car for smudged prints. They needed to concentrate their sneaking talents in other areas right now.

Taking his familiar place in front of a computer keyboard and a video screen, Wilson did a little investigation of his own.

When he typed in MICHAEL KNIGHT and ran the three sets of prints taken by Deke through the machine, he got a three letter answer: NIA. He frowned, then nodded. Okay: step two.

His first thoughts had been that Wilton Knight had sent some offspring to avenge the job wrought by Tanya on Knight Industries two years ago. But Knight had no children. The computers yielded no records of adoption or of legal wards. Wilson did not believe in coincidences and felt that their latest interloper coming in with the name of Knight was an ominous echo of the past. There was always the possibility that it *was* a coincidence; Wilson had accessed phone-company records and discovered dozens—no, *thousands*—of people named Knight in California. But the coincidence did not interest him; the possibility of a link to Wilton Knight and Knight Industries did. All Wilson wanted was the smallest thread of evidence connecting the two, and then he could go ahead and kill the man now. Otherwise he'd have to wait for Tanya to do it; she was interested in the car, and that interest was all that was keeping Michael Knight alive at this moment.

Wilson had another thought. What if the guy was some kind of self-styled engine of retribution, taking up the Knight banner just as the old codger himself dropped dead? Somebody with a Robin Hood complex? That would make him truly dangerous because his actions would be totally unpredictable. He frowned again. Nobody really believed in the withered standard of Might and Right anymore, did they?

It was insane, but a good possibility. Knight's walletful of bogus identity supported it.

There was no time to try and figure out the enigma of Michael Knight, however. Tanya's plan was at the crucial stage; introduction of the indestructible car into the equation at this late date would only delay things, possibly get them all caught. The best solution, as Wilson saw it, would be to kill Michael Knight—the sooner, the better.

But even Wilson did not yet know enough about the car to steal it. He had to get to Knight before Tanya did.

Wilson pushed back from the computer console, clicking the display off. He decided to wander down to the shops and see how the car was coming apart.

He found Tanya standing over a masked workman manipulating a blow torch. She saw him as he approached.

"Fred, you're not going to believe this . . .

or maybe you are," she said. "You *did* see the race."

"What is it?"

"Symes, here, has gone through three diamond drill bits on the hide of this thing. Not a mark. We can't even puncture the tires; it seems they're filled up with some kind of foam instead of air. They're flat-proof. I tried breaking the windshield myself, with a pair of vise grips. They bounced off. We haven't been able to even open this thing up to look at the instrumentation yet. About the only thing I can think of is tipping it over and getting a look at its underside, but everything down there is impact-shielded. Same material as the car body. And not a serial number in sight."

Symes cut the torch and pushed up his helmet. "It's just like she says, Wilson. This baby is impenetrable."

Wilson handed a page of computer printout to Tanya. "Here's what all of our computer resources have to say about Mr. Michael Knight—or whatever his name really is."

She frowned at the slip of paper. "What the hell does NIA mean?"

"No Information Available. And here's something else for your scrapbook. Microscopic examination of Michael Knight's fingerprints tells us that even those are as new as his credit cards. Sculpted by a real artist, but definitely fabricated prints. Probably plastic surgery on an incredibly advanced scale."

"That fits together with the car. All of this

rings a vague bell. We're missing a fact that should be obvious, Fred. I feel it." Now she looked worried.

He was surprised that Tanya could feel anything. "Don't tell me you're getting vibrations of woman's intuition at this stage," he mocked. He knew that would get him the sexism lecture.

But Tanya ignored it. "I mean it, Fred. We have all these tiny bits of information. They should make a picture, but they don't quite. We're overlooking something."

Wilson might have mentioned that he suspected the missing item was the connection between Michael Knight and Knight Industries, but he kept his lip zipped. It might not be wise to tell Tanya everything, considering the modifications of her game plan he had in mind.

"The scheme is unraveling," said Tanya. "Symes, keep plugging away at this thing. Get ready to pack up in a hurry if you have to."

Wilson drew her away quickly. "What are you talking about!" he hissed.

"Fred, somebody on a very high level is breathing down our necks. Maybe it's time to get out."

He ignored the fact that a few moments ago this had been his plan, as well. Instead he said, "You mean cut and run when in two or three days we'll have Com Tron's design specifications in our pockets?"

"I've already gotten the coded access numbers for the big one, the bubble-memory-chip design. I got it last night, from Benjamin."

"You mean he didn't give it to you but you got it."

This was not relevant to Tanya. "It's ours. It's the main item of information we're after. The other stuff is just gravy."

"You seem pretty flip over two or three million dollars worth of gravy."

"The bubble chip is worth more than all of Com Tron's other patents combined!" Tanya protested angrily. "We can pull it out of the computer and fly out of here with it tonight. Leave the country. Let the heat die down a bit."

"Tanya, you're in a panic over nothing. If this Knight guy had one scrap of hardcore evidence, would he be wasting his time with things like the demolition derby, or would he let himself rot in the Millston jail? There would be a whole pack of government dudes breaking their necks to get him out. Or he'd bypass the sheriff and let the authorities know he was locked up."

This did not calm Tanya down. "He's not an ordinary cop or government agent, Fred. He's far more dangerous."

"Another feeling?" That made two in one day, which was a record for someone with as cold a soul as Tanya's.

She nearly slapped him. Was he so stupid that he did not feel a sense of impending catastrophe? Behind them, an engineer in coveralls was vainly trying to wedge a crowbar into the door groove of the black automobile. When the crowbar began to bend under his weight with no sign of give on the part of the car, he gave up. Several others were still hacking away with oxyacetylene torches and high-speed drills. One fellow, frustrated, swung a fire ax at the hood. It glanced off with the blade dulled by KITT's crystalline finish.

"The car is a bad sign. And Michael Knight might be the end of us all," she said. "But while the car might provide us with ammunition, there's only one use remaining for Mr. Knight."

"Which is?"

"We need him to get us *inside* the car."

"And what makes you think he'll be so gracious as to simply hand over the keys when we ask him pretty please?"

Tanya sighed. She knew Wilson was toying with her, but did not quite know why. "You have that gorilla named Gray pick Mr. Knight up by the lapels and shove the barrel of his Magnum down Mr. Knight's throat. I think he'll let us see his car. After all, he was interested in selling it, or so he said." She turned and shouted. "Symes! Give it up. Let the boys knock off. Lock this thing up and put a guard outside for the night."

The workmen gladly dispersed. The car remained as it had looked when towed in.

Tanya checked her watch. "Okay. In two hours I want you to pull Michael Knight out of jail and bring him here. I'll need that long to make sure Benjamin is happy and to clear the design specs out of the computer."

"You're sure you want to cancel out now?"

"Who's running the Com Tron phase, Fred—you or me?"

"All right, all right." Let her have this round, he thought. It did not matter. Soon she wouldn't be running anything. "And what do you want to do with Knight, since you're giving the orders?"

"Kill him, of course. Now get to work."

10

It was dark and silent inside the Com Tron plant's number-two shop and garage. The engineers had buttoned it up for the night, and outside the padlocked rolling door of corrugated steel there was a sentry standing with his hands behind his back, chewing on a toothpick.

The door would be opened for one person only: Tanya Walker. She was due to show up with Benjamin's new security chief, Fred Wilson, and an unnamed third party in about an hour. The guard, whose name was Mikels, had been handed quite a few of these late-night assignments recently at time-and-a-half pay and didn't care about anything except pleasing Walker and Wilson with his performance. To Mikels, performance always equaled promotion. Once promoted, he could pick his own hours.

Com Tron, like any large factory facility, put out its share of atmospheric signature noises even when shut down for the night. Certain machines could not be turned off. If the computers were killed for the night they might dump data; in the case of the large mechanisms for parts fabrication and the pocket smelters used to purify metal components, it was often cheaper to keep them humming all night rather than fire them up fresh at the beginning of each workday. There was no nine-to-five shift at Com Tron, but three staggered eight-hour shifts that kept some people working away no matter how the hands on the clock read. Mikels, therefore, was accustomed to the circumambient noise of the factory complex.

But a new sound added itself to the general din, and he caught it immediately. It sounded very much like someone had started the engine of the car locked inside garage number two. That meant a trespasser, unauthorized personnel, and Mikels had very strict and specific orders.

He'd have to unlock the person-sized access door to check. He unsnapped the fastener anchoring his service revolver to the holster and pulled the ring of keys from the reflex reel on his belt. The tiny chain racheted out to full length.

Inside the engine revved, just once.

KITT's red sensor eye scanned the absolute darkness inside the garage.

Via long distance, Devon had fed the coordinates of the Killston sheriff's office into the microprocessing unit. The information was digested.

The interior video screens blinked on and hurried through a catalog of surface maps of the Millston area, selecting and programming the most likely route to the jail.

One screen recorded a 360-degree surface scan of the garage interior, logging it for reference. Using the distance relationships established by the scan, KITT computed space versus momentum potentials as required by the yardage to the rolling garage door.

X-ray scan revealed two weak bolts in the upper left of the doorframe and the caster mount for the door itself. That would require selection of an impact point at an angle convenient to make use of the weakened bolts.

The metal of the door was still radiating stored heat from a day's worth of sun, but the strongest concentration of heat registered by the infrared sensors occupied a more compact area about six by one and a half feet square. A man was standing outside: KITT's audio nets verified this by recording the sounds of respiration, heartbeat, a belch. The man maintained his position stiffly in front of the garage door, so KITT deduced that this must be a sentry.

Unless the man moved, KITT would be compelled by his programming to abort the escape plan Devon had fed into him. No matter what kind of aid Michael Knight might be in need of, KITT could not harm the man outside—and that would surely happen unless the man moved out of the path of the huge door that would come crashing down. The possibility of injury became too probable to dismiss.

The parameters of the garage were rapidly reviewed in case they might yield an alternate strategy. None existed. The big retracting door was the only way out. There was a smaller entrance but it was not big enough for KITT to fit through.

There was, however, the possibility of a diversion.

KITT's light hoods glided up like the phosphorescent eyes of a jungle cat opening at night, glowing powerfully as the headlamps came on. The door was bathed in hot glare. The engine turned over and idled.

Increased heart rate and adrenaline flow was recorded for the man outside. After a moment, the heat shape of the guard moved for the smaller door, leaving a blue residue of dissipated warmth trailing behind him.

The myriad readouts of the super dash blinked on. The gearshift knob shifted itself into first and the steering column monitor came alive with the bright blue lightbar of PURSUIT.

The heat shape was now neatly framed in the outline of the smaller doorway, out of the trajectory needed to take out the big door.

KITT's high-traction tires spun on the garage floor and the black car launched itself at the closed corrugated door. At the second before impact, turbo boost was applied at one-quarter thrust to provide penetration speed without shooting the car into the air.

The huge steel door broke free of its moorings and unfurled into the night like a huge amphitheater curtain clipped from its scaffoldings. It backflipped in KITT's wake, hurling sink bolts and chunks of shattered concrete in a wide fan, like shrapnel.

Mikels forgot about his gun long enough to shield his head from all the flying debris, then unholstered his piece and fired after the escaping car, to absolutely no practical effect. The caving-in door sounded like ten thousand frying pans clanging on the concrete all at once.

KITT hauled a suicidally sharp right-hand turn and disappeared east at better than 90 miles an hour.

Carney had returned to Michael's side of his own cell, and seemed repentant. His hands closed around the bars, and after making sure Michael was still awake, he spoke.

"Hey, cowboy. Hope you don't take what me and the boys did to you tonight too personally. We was all under orders."

"Looks like you took a few lumps yourself," said Michael. Right now he was grateful for another human presence, even if they had been at each other's throats a couple of hours previously.

"Yeah, you unpacked a few fancy moves, all right." He rubbed his throat where Michael had pegged it. "Where'd you learn to fight like that, anyway? You look like just another skinny cowboy that'd blow away in a strong wind."

"Military," said Michael.

"Shoot," Carney scoffed. "They sure as hell didn't teach us any moves like those in the army. You see any battle?"

"You might say that." Michael hated talking about his war years. Too much remained in his memory to make the recollections painless.

"Vietnam?"

"Right."

"You ever been in prison before?"

Michael thought of the jail tours he'd done while on active duty as a police officer and rejected the easy answer to Carney's question. "Yeah, once."

Carney was the sort of man who believed that everybody had a sin or two to hide, that nobody was clean, and Michael's answer pleased him. It put the two men on a more equal footing, he thought. "What'd you do to get tossed in the slam?"

"I was in army intelligence. The Cong snared me. I was a POW."

"Wow," said Carney with a kind of admiration. "One of the few who made it back. You escape or were you let go?"

"Escaped." A little dart of pain had appeared in Michael's forehead. He remembered cutting the Cong sentry's throat.

"What happened to all the gooks?"

"I had to punish them."

That shut Carney up for a moment. Then he said, "You got anybody on the outside? It doesn't look like nobody's gonna show up to let either one of us out."

"I have a friend," Michael clarified. "What about you? How come you're the only one from the bar that made it all the way to the jailhouse."

"Oh, yeah. Well, cowboy, you put some of those old boys in the hospital. Like Dolan, the guy who broke his head and the beer mug at the same time. You broke Farrell's arm falling over the bar. And Logan . . . that poor dude's gotta do some time in a dentist's chair. You relieved him of his front teeth."

"Yes, well, as you said, I hope they don't take it too personally. But why are you locked up in here and nobody else?"

Carney fidgeted. "Well, y'see . . . I'm sort of the scapegoat of the bunch. Old Deke the Geek couldn't just lock *you* up. That would attract attention, and Com Tron don't want nobody paying undue attention to them. So here I am. I'll get out tomorrow morning. I got a load to run down south, to the City of Industry. I'll be on time."

"You sound like you've done time in stir before."

"Yeah, I've got all kinds of little tricks to help pass the time. I prefer conversation, though. It's easiest to forget a long stretch when you're talking it out with someone else who ain't in no better shape than you."

"What about the other drivers, the guys in the race, the guys who helped pound me? They local boys?"

"No way. Com Tron imported us special. We all got hired by that new security guy, Wilson. Fred Wilson. My parole had just come through and I was getting ready to take my leave of San Quentin, and I get this phone call." Carney mimed holding a receiver and laughed. "I said what the hell. When I got out of prison there was three times as many unemployed people as there was when I went in. Wilson trained me to drive trucks. The first day I showed up at his office—the only appointment in my life I ever been on time for—he plunks two week's pay down in my hand, in cash. Hell, we get all kinds of overtime, plus regular pay for running components from Com Tron, plus a cut of the benefits, like medical and stuff. Guys like me, well, all we have to do is be available—"

"For the occasional extracurricular assignment," said Michael.

"We don't have to break too many laws."

"Sounds like the unskilled laborer's dream job. Ever wonder what an electronics firm needs with a private army of bully boys?"

Carney chuckled. "I don't get paid to worry about that, cowboy. I just do as I'm told."

"Somehow I thought you'd say that. Any idea of what time it is?"

"That's one of the guard games you get in jail. Nobody'll ever give you the time. You notice what time they brought you back in here from making your phone call?"

"No," Michael said, thinking it peculiar. He had looked at the clock in Deke's office but not noticed the time; he must have been more anxious to get hold of Devon than he thought.

"Well, I'd reckon it's been nearly two hours since then."

"That's uncanny," said Michael. "How can you be so sure?"

"When you do time, cowboy, time plays tricks on you. You learn to turn on your inner clock and trust it. It's been just about two hours."

Michael reclined on his bunk, lacing his fingers behind his head.

"Gettin' late," said Carney. "Even if your friend does show up, he may not be able to get you out till morning now."

"I don't know. My friend and I aren't on the best of terms."

"That's not so good. Better try to catch some shuteye."

"Yeah." Michael closed his eyes and tried to empty his mind of worry. Time could not move slower or faster. It always moved at the same pace, so he stopped trying to rush it along. He wondered if Devon was en route, and where KITT might be and what Maggie was thinking.

His eyes came open an indeterminate time later. It was quiet in the cell block, and Carney was snoring.

He heard a car outside building up speed.
That was his last clear image.

The solid brick wall against which he had
his back fell inward on top of him, his bunk
flipping and dumping him onto the stone floor.
It sounded like the Washington Monument
coming apart and burying him personally.
The flat steel of the bunk acted as a shield,
protecting Michael from most of the broken
brickwork that exploded toward the far wall
of the cell like a deadly blizzard of stone.
Cement dust clouded the cell and made everything fuzzy against the all-night light of the
mesh-screened bulbs.

He reacted fairly quickly, shoving the bunk
off himself. A cascade of shattered bricks slid
away to the floor, and he saw KITT's contoured prow jutting through the brand-new
hole in the cell wall.

Michael's mouth tried to say *I don't believe
it* . . . but nothing came out. KITT's pulsating
red sensor scanned him dispassionately, tracking right to left.

Carney was up and his eyes were wide. "God!
It's gotta be some drunk . . . check and see if
the dumb sucker hurt himself!"

Michael quickly picked his way over the
debris piled up against KITT's nose and the
driver's side door obediently popped open at
his approach.

"Wait a minute!" shouted Carney. "I don't
see nobody in that machine! Who the hell is
driving?"

*   *   *

Fred Wilson arrived at the sheriff's office a little after midnight. The drive from Com Tron took about a quarter of an hour through winding mountain hills; the drive from the sheriff's place to the municipal airport would take another twenty or so. He wondered if Tanya Walker was plotting to abandon him with Michael Knight in his custody, or whether she coveted the car badly enough to prolong their little business relationship after the Com Tron debacle. Wilson had no interest in Knight; he would just as soon leave the country with the top-secret Com Tron specs and forget about the car. But maybe Tanya was right.

Deke Bannerman was the only uniformed officer present at the station, and Wilson found him, feet up on his desk, perusing this month's centerfold. He was waiting for his deputy, Kyle, to relieve him and there was a slight indication of disappointment when he looked up and saw Wilson coming through the glass door instead.

"Evening, Deke," said Wilson.

"What can I do for you, Mr. Wilson?" Deke straightened himself out behind the desk. Deke loved to play lawman.

"Got a court order here for the release of one Michael Knight," said Wilson. "You're to remand him into my custody." Wilson produced a folded sheet of paper.

"Tonight? Now? Seems a little irregular."

Wilson laid the page on the desk; Deke did not bother to examine it. "Everything's in order, Sheriff, don't worry. Mr. Knight's em-

ployers have been in contact with us. Frankly,
I'm relieved that this whole unsavory situation has come to such a calm and anticlimac-
tic resolution, if you know what I mean."

Deke did not. He hated big-city words and
city-slicker types like Wilson, whose stream
of gobbledygook talk was most likely very
official and true—therefore making examination of the document unnecessary. He dug out
his key ring for the cell block and hoisted his
bulk out of the office chair.

"We'll see if the prisoner's awake," he said.

Then there was a horrendous, hollow *boom*,
as though a bomb had gone off in the rear of
the building. Plaster lath sifted down from
the ceiling beams, coating Wilson's suit coat
and Deke's tan uniform.

"What the hell was that?" said Wilson, fear-
ful of an earthquake tremor. They happened
a lot in this area, and he was certain the big
one would roll along at any moment. He had
always planned not to be around to witness
it.

Deke said nothing but fumbled his keys in
his attempt to open up the cell-block access
door. His trembling fingers finally selected
the correct key and jammed it home.

Both men ran down the short corridor and
rounded the corner leading to the cells. Wilson saw Michael Knight jumping into the black
car and knew instantly what had transpired.
While Deke stood aghast at the damage, Wilson hauled his pistol out from beneath his
armpit and cut loose three rounds in the di-

rection of the car. The gunshots were like cannon blasts in the enclosed cell block. The slugs skimmed harmlessly off KITT's hide, sparking like struck matches and ricocheting into the night.

The car sped backward before Michael even got his hands to the wheel. Another of Wilson's shots deflected off the windshield in front of Michael's face.

Wilson ran out, not caring about Deke or the damage or his other prisoner. He burst from the front of the building as the black car locked brakes and spun, turning itself around. Its taillights vanished over the hill before Wilson could even get his own security vehicle started.

He sped in pursuit but knew it was useless. Driving one-handed, he grabbed his CB mike.

"Gray! Gray, are you out there! This is Wilson!"

After a second, Gray's voice came over the box: "Gray here. What's up?"

"Michael Knight has regained possession of the car and is headed for Com Tron, as far as I can tell. I'm in pursuit but there's no way to match the speed of his machine. I want you to alert Symes and put some of our guys out on the road, in their rigs—just in case Com Tron isn't Knight's target."

"What if it is?"

"Then we don't have to worry. Our security is sufficient. Knight wouldn't have made the breakout if he didn't have any hard evidence, so I'm betting he knows about Tanya's plan and is really headed for the municipal airport to cut her off. Is she still at Con Tron?"

"As of ten minutes ago, affirmative," Gray said.

"Alert her. Knight is on his way but he shouldn't be able to infiltrate unless he drives straight through a wall—in which case we'll be right on him."

"Got it. What about you?"

"Marry up with me on the Post Road. We'll proceed directly to the airstrip. We are blowing Millston *tonight!*"

"Right. Gray out."

Wilson coaxed more speed out of his own vehicle, but the sleek black machine was long out of sight.

Michael could not remember even closing his own door. KITT was in complete control. The door slammed for Michael and the car burned rubber in a dead beeline backward for twenty yards, until there was sufficient clearance to orient forward. By then Michael had recovered enough to grasp the wheel. They pulled better than 100 per going over the first hill.

"KITT! How the devil did you find me?"

"Devon interceded with a rather well thought out contingency plan," responded the machine, its red voice light fluctuating. *"It's good to see you well."*

"It's pretty good to see you, too. Like the cavalry."

"By the way, might I inquire as to our destination?"

"Com Tron. I still haven't had my meeting with Tanya Walker."

"That could prove hazardous. Miss Walker's plan was to have you brought from the sheriff's office to Com Tron, where she would attempt to coerce you into letting the engineers examine me. There was also something about leaving the premises in a great hurry."

"Our appearance in Millston shook her up," said Michael. "She's either identified me or is nervous enough to try to grab what she can get and jump ship on Com Tron tonight."

"It is reasonable to assume that Com Tron has been alerted by now, you know."

"Yeah. Have you got anything in your magic hat that'll get me back inside the plant?" He thought of the spectacular jailbreak that had just taken place and added, "Uh—quietly?"

"Leave everything to me," said KITT. *"While I was secured in the garage, I scanned an architectural plan for the entire Com Tron plant and have preselected the most unobtrusive infiltration point."*

"I assume you got out the same way you got me out of the jail?" Michael was still coated with brick dust.

"The process was fundamentally the same, yes."

"What about your rule against harming people? You nearly buried me alive in my own private brick pyramid." Let him gnaw on *that* one, he thought, regaining some of his humor now that he was back in the game.

"I was able to scan your approximate loca-

tion with my infrared systems," said KITT. *"And the stress points in the wall were calculated to afford you the protection of your steel bunk when you fell. There was no perceivable error. As I have stated, the details of both escapes were essentially identical. No human life was jeopardized in either case."*

"If you say so." He could see the uppermost lights of the Com Tron plant already. They jumped another hill and the plant itself rolled into view.

"As for Miss Walker's plan, perhaps this excerpt will enlighten you," KITT continued. There was a pause, then Michael heard Tanya's voice on KITT's playback monitor: *". . . the bubble chip is worth more than all of Com Tron's patents combined! We can pull it out of the computer and fly out of here tonight. Leave the country."*

Then came Fred Wilson's voice: *"And what do you want to do with Knight?"*

"Kill him, of course." KITT had unobtrusively recorded everything while sitting in the Com Tron garage.

"Great," said Michael dully. "Edited highlights of the plot to murder me." He slowed the car. "KITT, how close can you get me to the place where Tanya is most likely to use the computer to access the bubble-chip design?"

"Already inserted into the plan," noted KITT.

"Excellent." He killed the headlights and ran on infrared, so the car's approach would not be noticed. "In that case, let's get in there and beat them to the punch."

The car glided silently down into Com Tron territory.

11

There was a single car parked in the executive lot of Com Tron, and the curbstone in front of it was labeled T. WALKER in black stencil. KITT coasted quietly up into the adjacent space.

Before the cars was a sheer stone wall, the west end of the factory wall itself. It ran straight up for nearly a hundred feet and was topped off with flanged lattices of razor wire to discourage any interlopers who felt like mountaineering up its clifflike surface.

Michael backed out and ran KITT parallel to the wall until they were away from the light of the mercury-vapor streetlamps. The northeast corner was just as high, and KITT informed him that there was a high-voltage electrical current running through the strands of barbed wire at the top of the formidable barrier.

"Wonderful. So how am I supposed to get past all this well-thought-out security? You ram through the wall and we'll be covered with guards before the bricks stop falling, and I've got to get to Tanya."

"Might you entertain a suggestion?" said KITT.

Michael's attention was attracted by another urgently blinking pushbutton.

PASSENGER EJECT/PILOT EJECT

"You're kidding," he said, then, in a queasier tone: "You're not kidding. . . ."

"If you adjust the pressure tubes for six hundred pounds of vertical thrust precisely, you should clear the wire and land quite softly—as if you'd dropped from an approximate height of five feet."

"What if I miss?"

"Trust me."

Michael twisted a chromium dial until a set of blue digitals read out 600 LBS/THRUST. It was too easy. "You mean all I have to do now is"—he swallowed—"hit the button?"

"It would help a great deal if you open the sun roof first," KITT added dryly.

"Not funny. We're talking about a hundred feet straight up."

"No, Michael—you're the only one talking about it. Your trajectory is angled so that you can't possibly fall back the way you go up. I'd advise ejecting now, before our presence is discovered here, or before you lose your nerve."

"Wise-guy car. I'll show you who's lost his bloody nerve!" Michael thumbed back the sun

roof and poised his finger over the red PILOT
EJECT button. Privately, he was extremely
grateful that Buddy had not discovered and
pressed this button during the race. He in-
haled a deep breath and held it in. "Wish me
luck, KITT," he said.

Genially KITT replied, *"Good luck, Michael."*

Michael pressed the button. There was a
vacuum rushing of air and the feeling of being
boosted skyward by an enormous padded
hand. The top of the wall grew to meet him.
He had to pull in his legs, but KITT's aim
hooked him neatly over the edge, and he
landed on a tar-papered roof on his hands
and the balls of his feet, surrounded by gigan-
tic industrial air-conditioning units.

A hundred feet below, the sun roof hummed
shut by itself.

Tanya Walker emerged from the push-bar exit
door at the far end of the corridor leading to
the executive offices. She was overlooking the
deserted Com Tron central yard below. Every
so often a sentry passed beneath a pool of
light and was swallowed up again by darkness.
She had just sent a guard out to check on her
own car in the wake of KITT's escape and Fred
Wilson's somewhat confused and panicky
report. Everything seemed to be falling apart,
and if need be she wanted to get herself out
intact. In her left hand she held a slim, burn-
ished transceiver, an executive version of the
bulky, black FM radio units toted by all the
Com Tron security staff.

She steamed. Why the hell hadn't Wilson shown up yet? And where had Wilson's henchman, Gray, vanished to? About the only operative she'd been able to reach on the FM box was Symes. She was about to check up on them all again when her radio buzzed. It was Mikels, the guard she had sent to check her car, and the man who had almost been crushed when the black mystery car chewed its way out of Com Tron's number-two garage.

"Miss Walker, you're not going to believe this . . . but it's back, and there's nobody in it."

Eyes flashing, she held the transceiver to her face. "What do you mean, it, Mikels! Make sense!"

"That haunted car," Mikels said. "It's back."

"Back where?"

"Right down here in the northeast corner of the parking lot. I was making sure your car was okay when I—"

"Never mind! Stay right there. I'm coming down!"

The night was getting chilly, but Tanya let her own growing anger warm her. Surely her gown was not substantial enough to keep the cold at bay. Yet that, too, had accomplished its purpose. No one would have to worry about tripping over Will Benjamin during the night's action. The first half of her job had been achieved. All that remained was to access the bubble-chip specs and get out as quickly as possible. If none of her cohorts could keep up with her schedule, then they'd have to lump it.

As she came through the gate, moving briskly, Fred Wilson's car sped hurriedly up. She jumped inside and directed him toward her own car at the end of the lot. Just behind Wilson was Gray, the assassin, inside a second car.

"Knight beat you back here, Fred," she said, letting her acid tone cut into him. "He's probably already inside."

"But he's not in his car, obviously," said Wilson. "So we've got a box around him. First thing that's gone right all evening, Tanya." He floored the brakes, making the security vehicle skid to a stop next to Michael's car. "Look. There's no way for him to get over the wall here."

"And there's no way for him to bust out of jail either, right?" She dismissed Wilson from her attention. "Mikels! You're to remain here. If anyone approaches the car without my authorization, shoot to kill. That's an order!" Then she grabbed the mike on Wilson's radio. "Attention all Com Tron security personnel. There is an intruder on the grounds attempting to penetrate and remove vital, top-secret data. This man conforms to the description of Michael Knight you've all been given. He is to be located and apprehended at once. If he resists, your orders are to shoot to kill. This is a crucial matter of national security. Com Tron's United States defense secrets are at stake. Repeat, apprehend and detain Michael

Knight at once. His mission here is harmfully contrary to the interests of national security!" She rehooked the mike. "That ought to do it."

"Do what?"

"Generate enough paranoia around here to permit us to escape during all the confusion," she said. "Now get me back to the gate, pronto. I've still got to get up to the ninth floor and access the data we need."

"You're giving up on Michael Knight? You should've done that this morning," Wilson said as he made for the main gate.

"I haven't," said Tanya. "If we haven't snared Knight by the time I finish upstairs, I'll go ahead of you to the airport. I'll expect you to show up with Knight in custody. Then we'll leave. You, Knight and Gray take the Com Tron chopper to the airstrip."

Gray was to be their pilot, so Wilson did not fear Tanya would betray him by leaving Com Tron first. The betrayal would come later, under less hectic circumstances.

"Have one of the guards move my car to the courtyard," she added, tossing a set of keys on the seat next to Wilson and getting out of the car by the gate. "And it's not too soon to have Gray warm up the helicopter." Then, with a grand swish of her evening gown, she was off.

Wilson used the spare moment to knock the empty brass from his pistol and reload. Just in case.

*   *   *

She moved quickly up the outside stairway and was inside the elevator within minutes, grinding slowly toward the ninth floor, where Com Tron's data-processing locus was. In the ninth-floor corridor she encountered Symes, the security man.

"Stay out in the hallway," she said. "Keep your eyes and ears open. I'll want you to escort me down. We'll be taking the jet out tonight." They hustled down the corridor side by side.

"It's on for tonight, then?" said Symes.

"Yes. Wilson should have Knight shortly. But if you're still here when he takes off in the chopper, Knight or no Knight, get out to the municipal airstrip as fast as possible." Symes was a good operative, and Tanya did not wish to lose him unless absolutely necessary for her own safety.

"Got it." Symes knew how to take orders. He unlocked the pebbled-glass doorway to the data-processing office and admitted Tanya.

Tanya rushed past the banks of video screens with their green standby dots pulsing patiently. She seated herself at the main terminal located at the far end of the huge room. The only light was from the screens and from the phone console an arm's reach away. She tapped in an identification code and the screen printed out READY.

Then she inserted the access and security codes. She had learned their location from Will Benjamin just an hour or so previously, and had obtained them in much the same way Lonnie had removed Charles Acton's secrets from the roof safe in Las Vegas. She punched a printout tab and Com Tron's design for the bubble-memory chip began to immortalize itself in black and white on green-lined graph paper.

As she sat waiting behind the desk, she hiked up her dress and removed the tiny Italian automatic from a soft calf holster on her right thigh. It was held in place by a very efficient garter. She snapped out the clip and checked the loads. The gun was quite warm.

She leaned over to check the printout and, seeing it was nearly complete, placed the gun on the desktop while she reached for the nearby phone and punched in a number.

She reached Wilson on his car phone. "Fred? In five minutes I'm out of here. I told Symes the plan. As for everyone else, you and I are jetting out on Will Benjamin's personal orders. Is my car set? Good. See you in about half an hour." She hung up and reached for her pistol.

A man's hand snaked beneath her own and snatched the weapon from her grasp while another hand curled over her mouth, yanking her violently back into the cushions of the desk chair.

"Very kind of you to organize all the evidence for me, Tanya," said Michael Knight, who had witnessed the whole job from the curtains by data processing's floor-to-ceiling bank of windows. Once into the building—he had used the central rooftop air duct as a crawl way—the registers conveniently placed outside the elevators on each floor told him where to wait for Tanya. The door had succumbed to Michael's lock-picking tool three minutes before Symes made his ten-minute circuit of the ninth floor. And Michael had waited.

Gently, he released her face and put the muzzle of the automatic in her ear. "One squeak," he said softly, "and your brains go flying out the picture window. Do you read me, Tanya?"

She nodded, still stiffened with surprise and fear.

"We'll talk for just a bit." Michael was enjoying Tanya's long-awaited comeuppance. He moved into the light, pointed the gun at her face from less than an inch away. "Or would you rather I paid you back this way? The setting's changed—no desert night, no stars—but I guarantee you it'll hurt just as much."

She looked past the silver gun, into his eyes, and her face blanched. "Michael? Michael . . . *Long*?" she said in a crushed voice.

"I'm a ghost," he told her. "I've risen from the grave to haunt you. And to pay you back on behalf of all the people you've walked on and worked over. And to make *you* pay. Your spy party is over, Tanya. Maybe a good, long stretch stamping out license-plate frames or learning barbering at one of our scenic state-supported penal institutions will give you time for reflection. Say thirty years or so. When you walk out, Miss *Walker*, you'll be a crone. Unable to face yourself even in a mirror. And that suits me just fine." Michael's teeth were clenched; he ached to kill her at that moment but knew that for Tanya, death would only be another kind of slick escape, with no suffering. He and others had suffered. There was a vast debt of suffering that would not be balanced by his losing control and blowing her away to get a second of perverse pleasure on behalf of a personal score. He held the gun steady. When her eyes weren't examining him, convincing her that this ghost really was Michael Long, they followed the pistol.

He expected her to squirm, and to grovel, looking for escape routes like a rat trapped in a maze, and as soon as she caught her breath she began.

"Michael," she said, averting her eyes from the gun and trying not to think of the curtain of orange fire that would explode into her face should it go off. "You don't want to do this. Not a man like you—a maverick. You must know that I didn't want to hurt you. You must also know that Fred Wilson would've shot you if I hadn't—and you'd be dead, now. I'd hoped you were alive even as we left. We all had orders. If anybody balked, there would have been two dead bodies out there at Tres Piedras instead of one survivor."

"You're babbling, Tanya. Uncomfortable?" He thumbed back the hammer on the small automatic and kept it aimed at her face. "Is that better? I hope not."

She didn't flinch, and he admired her nerve. "Things are different now," she said. "Wilson was giving the orders during the Consolidated Chemical job. But Wilson's getting obsolete. I'm going to need somebody—"

"To replace him," Michael finished for her. He knew the speech nearly word for word.

"Yes, exactly." She interpreted his understanding as approval, and went on. "With your mind, your looks, your resourcefulness, and things like that car of yours you and I could make an even more powerful team. All the money we extracted from Knight Industries, Consolidated Chemicals, RamCor Limited, Polex Corporation ... Michael—*all* of it is safely out of the country, in numbered Swiss and Belgian accounts." She let the implication hang between them.

"That's very tempting, Tanya, but you can't be trusted. You're one of those parasites whose word means less than nothing. It wasn't Wilson pulling the strings in Vegas, it was you. You're the only boss there is ... and you don't like sharing."

"All right, I'm the boss." She pressed her case. "But *you* know I could use someone with your talents. Not only could our relationship be *rich*, it could also be ... very rewarding as well." She shifted slightly in her chair, not threateningly.

She was really pouring it on, Michael thought— a performance that might well be worth her life if she could swing him over. He began to see just how power brokers like Acton and Benjamin had fallen for the routine: it was potent, and tempting. Complete freedom, millions of dollars, a beautiful woman . . . and the constant fear of a knife in the back. Most of her other marks had never reached that stage. But, he acknowledged to himself, even he might be seduced by such an offer, if he let it cloud his judgment.

"Not this time, Tanya," he told her. "You see, from now on, I work alone."

That was when Michael looked down and saw Tanya's foot touching the pedal-alarm trip beneath the desk. Symes's silhouette was already darkening the glass of data processing's door.

Michael moved, intending to get a forearm under Tanya's chin and use her and the chair as a deterrent or shield, but before he could get to cover Symes started firing with the practiced rhythm of a marksman. The first shot tore a furrow through the desktop, missing Tanya's stomach by inches. The second caught Michael high in the back as he dove, slamming him against the closed curtains while Tanya ripped away from him and hit the deck. Another shot blew a foot-wide hole through the window by Michael's head.

He returned fire with Tanya's Italian automatic and the pebbled glass of the door disintegrated like sparkling snow. Symes screamed and clutched at his chest, his pistol hitting the floor. Then he fell forward and hung limply on the door, his head and right arm protruding through the frame. His weight caused the door to slowly swing open, dragging him with it.

Michael's shoulder pounded with stinging pain. It felt like an ice pick was jammed there, immobilizing his left arm and making his hand humb. Holding the pistol in his right hand, he looked around for Tanya, but she had taken advantage of the opportunity to disappear.

His arm grated horribly when he tried to move it. Some bone had been destroyed by the slug, and already the area was swelling. He had to get out. The place would be overrun with guards in another second, and Tanya had slipped past him.

The sheet of computer printout was gone from the board. "Damn!" She had managed to grab it even while running for her life. Michael kicked open a fire door and emergency alarms began to wail throughout the building. He hopped down the stone stairway to the seventh floor. The noise would add to the confusion. As the door slid shut behind him he saw the shadows of guards dancing on the far end of the corridor.

"Hurry up, Harris!" said one. "You take accounting, I'll start with personnel, and we'll meet in the middle."

"Right!"

Michael ducked behind the first door that offered itself and waited in the dark. He heard the clinking equipment on the guard's belt mark his progress as he got closer. When the timing was correct, Michael attacked.

After fleeing the gun battle in data processing, the person Tanya collided with after rounding

the first turn in the hallway was a maintenance janitor in the employ of Com Tron. She
rebounded off the cart of cleaning materials
and nearly had a coronary in fright. Leaving
the janitor staring after her strangely, she ran
for the door to the outside stairs.

Once outside, she sucked in a calming
breath. She had actually been running as if
from a ghost, she thought with amazement.
Michael Long—or Knight—was only another
man, she knew, but she didn't plan on under-
estimating him even if (as she hoped) the security guards had him signed and sealed by
now. He seemed to have been hit by one of
Symes's shots . . . but then, he'd been hit by
bullets before, too.

Her car was parked below, waiting, and she
wasted no time getting to it and hot-footing it
for the airstrip. As she got in she flung the
crumpled wad of printout into the passenger
seat. She had her prize and a getaway was
hers in a matter of a few moments.

The further she sped from the building that
had Michael Knight in it, the safer she felt.

The security guard named Harris had just
passed by the door to the seventh-floor ladies'
room, checking the office alcoves, when a hand
wrapped around something metallic smashed
into his face. Harris folded up on the floor,
and the hand dragged his limp form quickly
into the bathroom.

Spots swam before Michael's eyes in the
darkness. He was losing blood fast. Removing

his jacket was painful; he simply tore his shirt away. The left sleeve and shoulder were deep red and glistening wet.

Stuffing a thickness of paper towels over the leaking hole in his back, Michael angled into Harris's shirt. The rest of the uniform followed except for the shoes; Harris had big, clunky size-E feet, and Michael kept his own boots. He strapped on the garrison belt with its pistol and cuffs and keys. Just then, Harris's FM unit spoke.

"This is Wilson. I want every guard to check in right now. From where in the building did the shooting come? Out."

Michael heard various men checking in and giving their locations. Wilson interrupted again: "Come in Symes, I want you to acknowledge right now!"

The walkie-talkie was silent for an instant. That was it. They'd swarm over the ninth floor in minutes.

Wearing Harris's uniform and gear, Michael stepped out of the ladies' room, tilting the cap to shield his eyes. He might just get away with it in the dark. He moved back to the fire stairs and closed the door just as Harris's partner came around into the main corridor.

Painfully, he made his way down seven more double flights of stairs, his heart pounding, his vision blurring. The exterior door through which he emerged to ground level was close to the main gate.

"Harris!" squawked Wilson's voice over the

FM unit. "Acknowledge, Harris; we don't know where you are."

He unclipped the unit and depressed the talk stud. "This is Harris. I'm covering the east wing of the eighth floor. Nothing to report."

He holstered the radio as he approached the gate. There was a single guard at the opposite side of the entrance, and they exchanged waves. Most likely the man was checking vehicles through the gate.

Then he saw the space where Tanya's car had been parked—empty. His own car was just around the northeast corner.

When he rounded it he saw the sentry keeping watch over KITT. "Hey, don't shoot," Michael said in a friendly tone. "It's me, Harris. Wilson asked to see you specifically over by the gate."

"Why didn't he radio?" Mikels was looking suspiciously at Michael. The lights from the factory gate obscured most of his features in an aura of glare.

"Something's funny with the walkie-talkies. Wilson says that this Knight guy has got some kind of jammer. It's fouling everything up...." He was almost to the car.

"Damm it," muttered Mikels. His hand moved to his FM unit just as Wilson's voice came over it: "Alert! Harris has just been found on the seventh floor, unconscious. His uniform has been stolen. Repeat: our suspect is walking around wearing Harris's uniform!"

Both Mikels and Michael went for their guns,

but Michael's wound restricted his reach. His shoulder felt like molten slag, burning and cracking.

"You hold short, man," said Mikels, gun up. "Don't move." He spoke into his FM unit. "This is Mikels. I've got our boy, dead bang, right out here by the car. He's wounded. He's not going anywhere that I can see."

Wilson's voice responded immediately. "You keep him right there, Mikels, and I'll personally put ten thousand dollars in your hands before another hour goes by!"

Mikels grinned. "Yes *sir*!" He cocked his hammer back for emphasis. Michael froze. "You almost made it, Knight," he said. "Pretty damned good . . . one man against a whole company. But you're all alone, now, and I gotcha."

"Except for my friend, behind you," said Michael, reaching slowly for his back pocket.

"Give me a break," snorted Mikels. "That's the oldest fakeout in the world. And there's nobody in the car. I know you can, like, start it by remote control or something. Big deal."

At Mikel's words, KITT's engine turned over and the brilliant headlights snapped on. Mikels stood fast.

"There's nobody in the car, Knight, knock it off or I'll blow you apart!" But he wasn't too sure now.

"Why don't you tell that to my friend," Michael said, still looking past Mikels to the car.

Mikels heard the door click open and could

not stand it any longer. He shot a glance backward. The door was open, but no one was there.

As he turned back—a movement that couldn't have taken more than a second—Michael put a slug from the Italian automatic he'd whipped up from his back pocket through the center of the badge on Mikel's hat.

Mikels sprawled back against the car, dropping his gun and grabbing at his head, which was still intact. *"Holy—!"*

"Hug the ground," Michael said, gesturing with Tanya's pistol. *"Now!"*

"Don't kill me," Mikels pleaded. "I got a sick mother. Two dogs at home. I got—"

"Just put your belly to the street and lace your fingers behind your head."

As he stepped past the prone Mikels, Michael heard Wilson, Gray and a cadre of security guards storm through the main gate. Wilson was waving his arms and yelling orders.

Michael almost screamed when the brown plush seat pressed into his back. He closed his door right-handed. The only way back to the highway was through Wilson and the men at the gate. He gripped the right side of KITT's wheel and put the pedal down. His blood began to stain the brown plush through the already-soaked guard's jersey.

Wilson anticipated Michael's charge and had two Com Tron security cruisers form a crash wedge blocking the only way out. Behind them, at least nine guards unslung pistols and rifles and began firing vollies toward the oncoming black car. Hot slugs skimmed off the hood and windshield, sparking. It was like barreling through a meteor shower, but KITT remained unscathed.

When the men saw that their bullets had no effect, they leapt from the path of the black vehicle as it bashed into the noses of the two cruisers. The right one screeched heavily around and hit a lightpole. Its companion flipped backward into the ground-level hot fence and exploded, hurling an orange fireball into the night sky and spraying flaming gasoline in KITT's wake.

Wilson shielded his eyes from the heat blast. Gray stood next to him, nonchalantly reloading his Magnum as though nothing had happened. Wilson grabbed a walkie-talkie away from one of the guards, who were now milling around, holding their useless weapons and waiting for a command.

"This is Wilson!" he barked. "How many of the truck drivers I ordered are still on the road?" One by one the truckers began to check in. "Stand by," he continued. "We may need you!" He turned quickly to Gray, who had reholstered his immense handgun. "Is the chopper ready?"

"Waiting for your order," said Gray.

"Let's move!" Wilson said. "We've got fifteen minutes to stop Knight before he reaches the airstrip!"

Gray jogged off to the Com Tron copter pad. Wilson considered all the men standing around him and, lacking any better directives, said, "Why don't you guys get to work and clean this damned mess up?"

Once again he jacked the empties out of his pistol, not quite knowing why he was even bothering to reload. By the time he reached the helicopter pad, Gray had the rotors up to takeoff speed. Their man-made vortex of wind flapped the coat of his "power suit" wildly.

"Get this thing into the sky!" he said angrily. Gray took hold of the throttle, and Wilson knew that if he could ever pry Michael Knight out of that damned black car, it would give him great pleasure to empty the pistol into his body, one shot at a time. That was a good enough reason for reloading.

12

"KITT? KITT? You there?" The black car weaved and Michael fought to reorient it on the winding road.

"Where would I go, Michael?" came the machine's reply.

"A million laughs," Michael said through dry lips. There was no mirth in his tone; he was struggling to remain conscious. He could feel Symes's bullet inside of him, grinding against broken bone and torn ligaments. He had soaked two shirts and the car seat in his blood, and was getting woozy. The fatigue from the last two days—the only rest he had gotten was an hour or two in the jail cell—intensified the effects of his injuries. But he kept himself awake and remained in control of the car. He had not gotten KITT's attention to take over. Not yet. Instead, he fumbled for words: "Look, KITT. I know we haven't gotten along all that well so far—that we've had some misunderstandings ... you know what I mean. I'm not sure I'm going to be around at the end of this trip. And I just—"

KITT's vital-signs scanner popped on instantly, noting Michael's statistics as the car interrupted him. *"You're suffering from extreme physical fatigue, shock, nausea and a gunshot trauma that could easily worsen. You require immediate medical attention. Your blood count—"*

"We can't stop, old buddy. They're going to be coming at us from all directions any second now." He thought for a moment, trying not to let the blur of white lines on the road hypnotize him. "Is there any way we can get in touch with Devon?"

"He is currently en route to Millston aboard the Knight Two Thousand jet."

"You mean there's a jet that does the things this car—I mean, that *you* can do?"

"I don't know, Michael. The data on the Knight Two Thousand series is classified information. You could reach Devon quite easily by radiophone and ask him."

"Do it. Do it fast."

An emergency buzz tone filled the car. Michael realized KITT was piping the call through the interior monitor speakers so he would not have to remove his good hand from the wheel. He was still in control.

Devon's voice came over the audio output: "Michael? What in the name of heaven is going on down there? We left the airstrip here just five minutes ago, assuming you were dead!''

"They *almost* killed me, Devon. They may yet succeed. If KITT hadn't showed up, I'd certainly be a goner by now.''

"Tell me what's wrong,'' said Devon.

"Mr. Devon, if you'll direct your attention to the vital-signs readout I'm transmitting, you'll see that Michael has been injured, is losing blood and his vital signs are deteriorating rapidly. My recommendation is that he should relinquish control of the car and allow me to take him to the nearest medical facility.''

"I'm not relinquishing anything!'' Michael grunted. The conversation seemed to be between Devon and his machine, and that infuriated him. Anger kept him awake, gave him the vigor to shout at the speaker.

"Michael, forget about Tanya and her sordid rabble,'' said Devon, clearly worried after seeing the duplicate readout on Michael's physical condition. "We'll regroup. Fight them another day. Wilton Knight's dream for you goes far beyond this one incident—''

"No, Devon, *you* forget it! Tanya and all the evidence against her are finally in the same place. I had her and she slipped away. They ripped off Com Tron—Symes, Tanya, Fred Wilson, Gray—that whole crew of pirates from the Vegas job. And they're leaving the country *tonight*. There's no time left. By the time you get to the Millston airport there'll be nothing for us to do but play cards and remember how stupid we were to let them slip past us!''

"If they're in possession of the evidence," said Devon, "I can have the local police intercede."

"Forget them. They've been bought off. Get in touch with an FBI or CIA unit; have them standing by. They can chopper in to the Millston airstrip in about the same time it'll take you to get here. It's my responsibility to stop them *now* so you can pick them up later . . . you read me?"

The car suddenly drifted short of a curve in the road, clipping away some of the cliff-side shoulder on the right side. Michael shook the cobwebs out of his head and corrected.

"That wasn't very graceful, Michael," said KITT in his usual sardonic tone. *"I really think you should let me—"*

"Shut up!" Michael straightened out his trajectory. "Devon? I'm really sorry about fouling up your plans—yours and Wilton Knight's. But I'll be damned if I'm not going to take us all out winners. . . ."

"He's manifesting his death-wish tendencies again, Mr. Devon."

It was an uncomfortable echo of Devon's own thoughts when he had been informed of Wilton Knight's selection of Michael as the human factor in the Knight-2000 test program. But Devon ignored it. "KITT—can Michael make it in his current state?"

"If you mean make it to the hospital, yes, I can offer somewhat mediocre odds for his survival. Since he has not vocalized his intended plan, however, I cannot speculate further. The

readouts speak for themselves. He's in bad shape."

"Michael!" said Devon. "I forbid this! You'll destroy everything!"

"Maybe," said Michael. "You're going to have to trust me, aren't you, Devon?" He had to keep talking, stay conscious. "There's one more thing that gripes me."

"Yes?"

Michael spoke right into KITT's monitor screen. "I don't like having anything to do with a car that can take off all on its own, that listens to my thoughts and makes its own decisions."

"You're giving it far too much credit."

"I don't think so. I can see myself out on a dance floor sometimes . . . and my car comes up and cuts in on me."

"Amusing, but not factual," said KITT. *"I have no supernatural powers, Michael. The reason you believe I can 'read your thoughts,' as you put it, is merely due to programming that specifies—"*

"That will be quite enough, KITT," Devon said.

KITT obediently clammed up.

"Your boy about to spill some important secrets about me?" Michael said, more alert because he was more angry. "Come on, Devon, what's the big bloody secret?" His one hand tightened on the wheel. The other felt . . . nothing. His entire arm was numb and cold.

"Keep him talking, KITT," said Devon. "Keep

him angry, if that's what it requires to keep him alive!"

"I don't know if what I have to relate will actually anger Michael further, but I do feel he needs to know—"

"Know what, KITT? Tell me."

"Approximately five hundred yards in front of us there is a large vehicle parked across the roadway. There is no access on either side. It is clearly intended to prevent further progress on our part."

"What was that?" said Devon.

"Com Tron's whistled their trucking fleet out onto the roads," said Michael. "That's how they're going to keep us from reaching the airport in time."

They rounded the final bend and saw the huge semi trailer truck dead ahead.

Devon was shouting into the phone link but Michael was not listening.

Wilson clapped a headset on as the Com Tron chopper tipped upward into the air.

"Who've I got out on Route 17?" he shouted against the eggbeater noise of the rotors.

There was a burst of CB static. "This is Dugan. I'm two miles shy of the Curson cuttoff."

"This here's Red Watson. I got my rig headed south on 17 just shy of the turnoff to the McQuade farm."

"Dugan!" said Wilson. "I want you to put that truck across the road near the Birch Street fork. Shove it right up next to the place where the road is carved through the side of the hill so Knight can't go around you!"

"Will do."

The terrain below them made following the roadway hazardous and shaved vital minutes away from the otherwise short hop to the airstrip. Wilson was more concerned with nabbing Knight; with that done, getting to the private jet would be less urgent.

"Here he comes!" came Dugan's voice. "He ain't even slowing down!"

"Is there clearance under the truck?" said Dugan.

"No way! He'll have to go right through me! And I'm bailing out!"

A horrific crashing noise spat out the earphone, making Wilson wince. He yelled into the throat mike: "Dugan! Come in! Did you get him? Dugan!"

When Michael saw Dugan's trailer blocking the road ahead of him, he pushed up his knee to steady the wheel while his hand reached for the TURBO BOOST button.

"*Michael,*" warned KITT. "*I'm not certain that the G-press of a full-strength firing of the turbo-boost function would be the best idea, considering your physical state.*"

"Let's find out, shall we?" Michael pressed the pedal down. Speed accumulated on the digital readout.

"*Michael, with all due respect—*"

"Quite! Give me a countdown on the distance!"

"As you wish." A rapidly changing set of blue digitals appeared on the super dash, enumerating the distance in meters to impact. The numbers were going too fast to watch. *"Mr. Devon? Isn't there some way you can rationally convince Mr. Knight that this is a foolhardy and reckless—"*

"KITT!" Michael shouted. The machine stopped talking. His finger stabbed the TURBO BOOST button. Then the steel flank of the trunk's box was flying at them.

The giant truck rocked back on its starboard wheels when KITT pierced the box like a black missile. Just a bit more thrust would have flown them completely over the obstacle but the effect was the same. Riveted metal screeched apart like tinfoil and KITT landed back-wheels-first on the far side. The jarring smash of recontact with the roadway wrenched Michael's muscles and clicked his teeth together. He tasted fresh blood in his mouth.

He ached, but his pain was delicious with victory. "I gotta admit . . . this car isn't too shabby!"

"Bold of you to admit it," said KITT.

"Don't rile me," he said to the glowing red screen.

"But according to you, Michael, to rile you—as I understand the meaning of the term from my information banks on slang and unconventional English—should improve your condition drastically . . . as illogical as that sounds."

Michael's fragile grip on consciousness seemed to flutter, then stabilize. His blood loss could not be balanced by the angry rush of adrenaline. "KITT, can you get me a patch-in on their radio communications?"

There was a scrabbling noise, then the clunk of the mike being lifted. "Dugan here."

"Well? Did you block him?" Wilson said impatiently.

"I blocked the road, if that's what you mean," clarified Dugan. "He smashed right into me."

"Good work."

"Not quite. He hit me, all right. Went clean through the trailer box like it was made out of Styrofoam. The truck's wrecked. And Knight's gone. . . ."

Wilson grit his teeth, remembering the mystery car's peculiar aerodynamic capacities. "You idiot!"

"You're not gonna stop that damned car, Mr. Wilson. You'd need a tank. Or a mountain."

"Red! Red Watson! You still out there?"

Red's voice came back. "Yeah. About ten miles from where Dugan got pasted. I heard the whole thing. I'm not going to be stupid. You'll just lose another truck."

Wilson's face was florid. "I want you to ram that black car! Head-on! A fifteen-thousand-dollar bonus is yours if you stop him! Do you read me?"

"What good is fifteen grand if I'm dead? Nobody could survive a head-on collision at that speed—not even in a truck!"

"Jump clear, you moron!" Wilson virtually screamed into the mike, his voice going high and girlish in rage. "He'll be going fast enough to kill himself! Jump clear of the truck and make sure you nail him! Twenty-five thousand dollars!"

Red was about to say forget it when Wilson tacked on the extra ten grand. Instead, he looked at the headlights whipping over a distant hillock and said, "Consider him nailed, Mr. Wilson. Sir."

The mountain dropped away beneath Wilson and Gray as they flew over the rise. Wilson could already see the Christmas-tree lighting adorning Red's trailer rig. After backtracking along the route he guessed the road took in the dark, he spotted Michael's smaller headlights, blasting along the road full-speed.

"Get down there!" Wilson shouted to Gray as the two sets of lights below converged on each other. He wanted a ringside seat for the wipeout.

KITT put through the eavesdrop patch, and Michael overheard the tail end of Wilson's order to Red Watson, driver of the second truck.

"Twenty-five thousand bucks," repeated Michael. "That trucker will do it even if he's scared white. Did you copy that, Devon? You still with us?"

"I'm afraid so," said Devon through the intercom.

"You know KITT's limitations better than

anyone. Can it—can *he* take a truck, head-on, and make it?"

"*I'd be interested in knowing the answer to that one myself,*" said KITT.

"I can't quite recall having put him to that precise test," Devon said ruefully. "I doubt that the vehicle would be totally undamaged. It would make a fascinating field test, however. Perhaps you could—"

"Never mind!" said Michael. "Terrific. He wants to use us *both* as guinea pigs, KITT."

"*Mr. Devon is first and foremost a scientist.*"

"So I've noticed."

"*A helicopter has just moved into range behind us,*" KITT added, just as matter-of-factly. "*The transmissions to the pilot of the truck now approximately one and one half miles ahead of us originate from the helicopter. And personally, I would prefer reaching the airstrip to reaching the truck.*"

"Michael!" said Devon. "I really must insist you put KITT on auto cruise. His maneuverability and reaction time will outstrip yours. You're in no condition for such high-speed moves!"

"Sorry, Devon. But Wilton Knight believed in the strength of the individual. Let's put that to the test, instead of KITT's indestructability."

"*In this case, they equal the same thing,*" said KITT. "*Regrettably.*"

"Have a little faith. We got past the first truck, didn't we?"

"Correction: we got through the flimsiest part of the first truck."

"KITT, I'm afraid that as long as Michael is in the driver's seat, and conscious, we have little choice."

"Right," said Michael. "You override me and I'll just punch the buttons back in manually. Hang tight; I can see the truck now, coming over the rise at ten o'clock."

The eleven-ton truck and the sleek black car charged at each other in the same lane, head-on. KITT's speedometer jumped into three digits.

"Any last words, KITT?" said Michael. "Parting shots?"

"I sincerely wish you hadn't put it tha—"

"Look!" said Gray, from the pilot's seat inside the Com Tron chopper. "That's the access road to the airstrip, down there on the left!"

Wilson snatched up a pair of infrared binoculars and investigated as the car and truck began to speed toward each other. "Yes it is. Even money which one of them gets there first."

"Nobody survives a high-speed, head-on collision with a semi," said Gray. He reached behind him and unracked a twelve-gauge automatic pump shotgun and laid it across Wilson's knees. "But just in case he does, try this."

Wilson lifted the riot gun and jacked a shell into the chamber. Then his hands returned to

the binoculars as the space between the two
converging vehicles was reduced to nothing.

"Knight's skidding! He's slamming his brakes!

He's done for!" he yelled exuberantly.

Michael waited until the truck's monster headlights threatened to swallow them and then
hit the brakes, spinning the wheel one-handed
and sliding into an elaborate "brodie" turn-
around. The front bumper of the truck connected with the rear one on KITT, but it was
not a hit—it was a glancing blow of impact.
KITT shuddered as the truck scraped past on
the right side and continued lumbering along
the road behind them. Red had leapt from
the passenger side three seconds before impact,
and was rolling head over heels down the
embankment on the far side of the road.
His truck continued on like a locomotive on
low steam, until it came to the curve in the
road. Then it uprooted the guardrails and
rolled two hundred feet downward, into a dry
creek bed, where it flopped over on its side
and died with a crash.

Michael opened his eyes. Devon was shouting over the radio. He looked at KITT's screen
and said, "Have any more faith in your fellow
. . . uh, man now?"

"I'm glad I don't have an organic heart,"
said KITT.

"Can't shave it any closer than that, now
could you?"

"Tell me about it. Later. Right now the heli-

copter is descending on us in what definitely seems like an aggressive trajectory."

Michael put the car back into motion, blazing up the one-lane road toward the airstrip. "Then let's go! We still have to stop them from hooking up with the jet!"

The chopper swooped into a low parallel path above the car, and Wilson commenced fire.

"Match his speed!" said Wilson. "It's up to us to at least slow him down, now!"

Gray obeyed, keeping the machine dead steady as Wilson leaned out of the open cockpit bubble, braced one foot against the landing runner and began to pump ear-shattering loads in the direction of Michael's car. Each shot rocked the copter with recoil.

Suddenly, a stinging spray of return fire salted the chopper with pellets. Spiderweb cracks blossomed on the canopy. Projectiles ricocheted around inside the cabin. And ominous black smoke began to chug out of the rotor housing.

"He hit us!" Wilson said, grabbing at his face where a pellet had torn it open.

"No, *you* hit us!" Gray growled, with genuine anger. "Your shots are bouncing back from the hide of that damned bulletproof car!"

"Make another pass! I'll get him point-blank through the window!"

"Forget it," said Gray. "You want to make yourself another pass, go ahead and jump out.

It's hard enough to run this close to the ground without hanging up on something; now we're damaged. We'll be lucky to make the airstrip ahead of him.'' He pulled the chopper up and put on more speed. KITT shrank behind them.

Wilson's shoulder sagged. He placed the shotgun back on his lap.

13

Tanya Walker had Lonnie and the others wait inside the small private jet. She waited outside on the tarmac, leaning against her parked car. Inside the jet, the Com Tron printouts and other stolen data were spread across the cocktail bar like a picnic lunch of illegal information.

She stamped out another cigarette, then looked up to see the Com Tron chopper listing her way, trailing smoke. It touched down—roughly—next to the car, and Wilson and Gray were shouting at each other. She ached to leave them both behind for the authorities but needed Gray to pilot the jet. Wilson she did not need for anything anymore, except to answer one question.

Gray jumped out as soon as both runners of the helicopter touched ground and sprinted for the jet. His Magnum bobbed wildly beneath his coat as he ran.

Wilson unbuckled and stepped down as Tanya dashed up to him.

"Well," she said breathlessly. "Did you take care of Knight?"

He laughed bitterly. "Does it look like we got him? The chopper's shot and he's destroyed two more trucks. I'm surprised he's not here already. Now, come on—we've got to roll!"

He started for the plane but Tanya did not follow him. He still held the riot gun butt-first in one hand. "What's wrong?"

"We're not leaving until I finish off Michael Knight."

At the mention of the name, Wilson saw the headlights of the Knight 2000 kick apart a parking-lot barrier and make a beeline for the jet.

Wilson grabbed Tanya's forearm painfully and practically threw her against the fuselage of the jet. "You imbecile!" he yelled. "You're just going to screw around and get us all arrested!" He hustled her up the ramp and into the plane. He did not have to use the riot gun, but its threat seemed enough to convince her. There was still a smear of blood on his face.

"Gray!" he said as he heaved the hatch shut and cranked the locking mechanisms. "Get us out of here now!"

They all felt the brakes disengage and the jet started to roll. Lonnie was slumped in one of the couches, looking like she had run all the way to the airstrip. Tanya was obviously unstrung with hatred. Wilson's face was dappled in sweat and blood, his power suit ruined by grime, smoke and scorch marks from the explosion of the security car back at the Com Tron plant. They did not look at all like the hardy band of corporate pirates, with the sneering, upper-crust image they had fashioned for themselves. Michael Knight had nearly dismantled them, single-handedly. One man! It seemed impossible. But Wilson had lived through the thrashing Knight had inflicted on them all and was now glad to be getting away with his skin intact . . . if not his suit.

He looked at the plans scattered across the top of the bar. Was any of this stuff worth *dying* for?

"You didn't kill him," Tanya mumbled, her eyes defocused. She was sitting in another of the revolving executive couches.

Wilson placed the riot gun on top of the plans. "You didn't either, Tanya," he said simply.

She nodded. "Later. When we're safe and some time has gone by. A man like him won't be too hard to locate again, not with our resources, our computer links. We have all his identification and credit-card info. It should be easy. In six months, or a year, we can come back and kill him." Her eyes lit up. "Slowly and painfully."

Acceleration pressed her back into the couch as Gray opened up the throttles. Wilson tottered unsteadily and grabbed the door to the captain's cabin for support. He stuck his head in. "Are we okay?"

"Knight's right behind us," said Gray, pointing his thumb backward. "Making good speed. If he really lays it on he might be able to put the car across our nose wheel before we can get it off the runway. If he manages that, we're done for. And do me a favor, Wilson."

"What?"

"Don't tell me he's not crazy enough to try it."

Wilson leaned across to look out the port window. The black car was trailing along just aft of their wing. The jet was picking up speed; he'd never make it to the front of the plane and get far enough ahead to turn into its path. He agreed that perhaps Knight *was* suicidal . . . but he would not get another opportunity to kill himself. The jet was moving too fast.

Wilson blew Knight a mocking kiss from the pilot window. Even at that distance he could see Knight was severely injured. Blood coated the shoulder of the guard's uniform he had stolen.

He was walking back into the main cabin when the jet lurched sideways, sprawling him onto the carpeted floor just as takeoff speed was reached.

Not even the unique sensation of Wilson's shotgun pellets spattering harmlessly off KITT's hide inches from his own face was enough to keep Michael from passing out due to blood loss and exhaustion. His system had passed beyond the point where mere danger or an imminent threat to his life could provide another reliable spurt of energy. He was a kind of robot himself now—locked onto a single goal, chasing that goal at all costs and not ceasing motion until that goal was achieved.

He asked KITT to slide down the windows so that the cold night air whipped through the car to shock his skin pleasantly and provide an ounce more of wakefulness. It made little sense—as KITT might have pointed out—physiologically, but it was a psychological trick Michael had come up with for use during long cross-country drives. It had developed into the kind of habit his body responded to automatically. When the car windows went down, his eyes opened fully. Pain was seeping back into his left arm, asserting itself and displacing the arctic numbness. The pain denied him the bliss of unconsciousness.

Michael did not even see the small drop gate with the flashing yellow light barring his way. All he saw was the jet on the small municipal runway and the people scrambling into it. KITT blew through the token security gate.

"Michael, my calculations indicate that although we should be able to match the taxi speed of the plane, we will not do so in time to block it, nor can we follow it into the sky. Not even at my top speed."

The hot, gritty blast of the jet turbines momentarily fogged the car's windshield. KITT compensated and the glass cleared "Pour it on," Michael said. "Run us parallel to their wingtip; that's all the distance we'll need."

The car accelerated in a black blur until the revolving blue wing light was blinking in Michael's face. He made out figures in the cockpit looking back at him, and the jet increased speed. A third of the runway was gone already.

"You're not thinking of cutting under their big wheels," said KITT in a decidedly sickly tone of disapproval. *"Are you? We'd most likely kill everyone in the plane. My basic programming directives would prevent the turn into the wheels. Michael, are you listening to me?"*

Michael closed up the distance between the car and the wingtip. He shouted—as much of a shout as he could manage—over the jet wash of air ripping through the interior of the car. "Don't worry, KITT, just hang on! We're about to take off!"

"Oh, no. Not again."

Michael stabbed the TUR80 BOOST button one last time.

KITT arced into the air at full thruster force. The wingtip was no match for the sophisticated Knight Industries alloy, and KITT's contoured nose neatly sheared away a large portion of the wing itself. Michael shielded his face unnecessarily as the damaged chunk of the jet's left wing bounced away behind them.

The pilot locked the wheels into a crash skid, reversing flaps to provide a drag on his remaining wing for more braking power. Michael stomped on his own brakes simultaneously. The plane slid hard to the left, tires smoking. The right-wing landing gear snapped off like a twig and the fuselage impacted with the runway, still sliding, as Michael's car slipped along inside the wide crescent gouged into the runway by the jet. There followed a sparking explosion, and the stump of the left wing detached and detonated, hurling hot metal and flaming gasoline in miniature repetition of the still-sliding plane's arc. It reminded Michael of napalm.

The jet finally stopped about fifty yards from the car. Now that the car was not moving at all, extreme fatigue overwhelmed Michael. He wanted to pass out . . . but the sight of the emergency escape hatches on the plane swinging open kept him on the rim of consciousness for a moment longer.

When the jet dropped to the runway, broke its wings and started skidding wildly, everyone aboard flew into panic. Except Gray. It was his job to dominate the machine when it misbehaved or tried to assume control, even accidentally. He called up every evasive-action trick he knew from his combined military and private flying experience. He managed the feat of ditching what was left of the port wingtip before the gas tanks blew. It bounced away behind them and burned. He assumed the right landing gear was going to break off, and it did. Gray's expert actions and icy calm ensured that the crippled jet would slide around broadside and stop exactly the way Michael witnessed it from his distant car.

Behind him Gray heard the passengers moving for the emergency exits. Wilson grabbed the stolen Com Tron plans and shoved past everybody in his haste to get them outside, to safety. But how were they going to run now?

Somebody shouted that they should run for the hangar.

Calmly, methodically, Gray unbuckled and got out of the pilot's seat. The panic stop had been as clean as possible, and he admired his own handling of it.

He had just stepped through the cabin door and was facing the emergency exit Wilson had used when the plane simply blew up all around him. Hot petroleum fire consumed the cylindrical interior so quickly that Gray had no time to suffer. He was dead in three seconds, and in the fourth the sheer heat made the bullets in his holstered Magnum explode.

Michael did not know it yet, but the death of his old partner Muntzy had just been avenged.

"Run for the hangar!" yelled Wilson. "We've got to find another way out!" He had thought fast and swept up the Com Tron blueprints. Tanya's thoughts had been on the riot gun, and Wilson saw her cradling it against her hip as their jet, their ticket to freedom, consumed itself with a noisy explosion.

She began to walk toward the black car

parked some fifty yards distant. Wilson moved after her. Several of the stolen printouts fluttered out of his hands, littering the runway.

"Hey! What are you doing?"

There was a slightly mad cast to her eyes. "I'll get us a way out of here that nothing can stop," she said.

"Tanya, come back here!"

"Shut up, Fred, unless you want to swallow some buckshot."

Wilson stopped halfway between the plane and the car. Tanya could no longer be reasoned with. She had not seen how ineffectual the ugly automatic shotgun had been against KITT scant moments before. Instead of entreating her further to stop, his attention turned toward the helicopter hovering above them in the sky. Its carbon-arc searchlight lit up the scene in a huge oval of blue-white glare.

Back at the splintered drop gate far behind them, several unmarked government cars whooshed through, their magnetic bubble lights blinking. They made time toward the crash site in a flying-wedge formation, bouncing onto the far edge of the runway.

Beyond the chopper Wilson saw the pinprick lights of an approaching jet floating in the black night sky.

I'd give anything to be up there, he thought, letting the rest of the now-useless Com Tron plans fall from his grasp. They covered his shoes like giant snowflakes.

He was not particularly interested when he heard Tanya scream.

*   *   *

Michael sagged in his seat. He had seen something inside the jet blow all to hell, filling the passenger windows with orange flame and causing smoke to coil upward from the open hatchways. He watched Tanya Walker running toward him from the wreck. Fred Wilson was close behind her, clutching an armload of fluttering papers. Tanya clutched something else as she ran.

His good hand dropped from KITT's wheel, limply. He tried to remember where he had stowed Tanya's silver pistol. He tried to reach for the holstered weapon he had stolen from Harris, the guard whose uniform he was messing up with blood. But neither of his hands would obey his brain now. His vision began to phase out. He was totally helpless.

He could not even summon the strength to close the window. He sat there dully, recognizing the object in Tanya's grasp as a riot shotgun and realizing that history was about to repeat itself.

When she came abreast of the car, she saw Michael Knight slumped in the driver's seat, probably already dead.

She was aware of the oncoming police cars, of the helicopter that would most likely land and airlift them all away to prison. She dismissed them from her mind. Even more than the escape the black car could provide, she wanted to kill Michael. To watch him die at her hands. To correct what she had fouled up so badly the first time, to rectify the mistake that had returned to haunt and destroy her life.

She shouted, straining her voice. "Are you alive? Are you awake? I want you to feel this!"

Disappointment commenced in her. Then she saw Michael's eyelids flicker.

"You still with us?" she asked in a more solicitous voice.

Michael's voice was dry and labored. "Tanya . . . ?"

She hoisted the riot gun, bringing the abbreviated barrel to bear a scant two feet from the window. He didn't have a chance. "You lose, Michael!"

"Tanya, no . . . don't . . ."

She smiled and pulled the trigger just as the driver's side window shot up with the speed of a guillotine blade. Michael saw the deadly flock of shotgun pellets smash flat against the unbreakable glass . . . and fly back the way they had come, in exactly the way the bullet at Tres Piedras had rebounded from the metal plate in his skull.

Tanya's face vanished.

She arched backward and fell onto the runway clutching at her head. Blood pumped between her fingers and began to spot the runway. She writhed on the ground, screaming, as Fred Wilson ran to her.

Bile rose in Michael's throat. He looked down and saw one of Tanya's high heels lying on the pavement where she had been standing.

The force of the shotgun pellets that destroyed her face had knocked her out of her shoes.

No longer deadly, he thought. And no longer lovely.

"KITT . . ." he whispered. "It's all yours, now. Take care of it. And KITT?"

"Yes, Michael?"

"Thanks."

The dash converted to the auto-cruise mode and the gearshift lever put the car into first.

The last thing Michael saw before blackness enveloped him was the light pattern of the Knight 2000 jet, coming in for a landing on a secondary runway.

14

The events involving the hospital never resolved themselves to more than a vague blur in Michael's memory. He remembered the lights around the emergency entrance and climbing out of the car under his own power. He could recall weaving on his feet for a little more than one second ... before collapsing into the arms of an orderly who stood outside sneaking a cigarette. The orderly had almost missed the catch. The cigarette had dropped from his mouth when he saw Michael's car drop him off, then cruise away ... under *its* own power.

The nightmares were worse than the pain. While asleep and under medication Michael dreamed he was reliving the incidents that had taken place in Las Vegas. Muntzy had gotten outfoxed, and Michael had ridden off to his own doom with his murderer sitting in the car seat beside him. Indeed, he had given her a lift to the death site. Michael was nothing if not accommodating.

Then came the betrayal, and the flash of orange, followed by a haze of blood red, then opaque blackness.

Except that as Michael felt the disfiguring bullet smash into his face, he also saw it happen from a different angle, with the dual point of view peculiar to dreams. Suddenly he had become the observer, not the victim. He saw Tanya grab her head and fly backward, her face—that regal combination of perfect features he had reflected upon in the casino, so long ago—obliterated. He experienced the pain as it happened.

He wondered if Tanya was in some other room in the same hospital. *Hospital?*

Michael's eyes rolled open. The glare from the soft fluorescent lights in the room caused him to slam them shut immediately.

"Hey? Anybody in there?"

It was a woman's voice, and Michael's hand automatically moved to find and grasp a gun that was not present. A smaller hand closed around his own wrist with gentle pressure.

He opened his eyes again and saw Maggie leaning over him, a concerned expression on her face.

"Hi," he said, weakly.

"I think you were having a bad dream," she said, then added with a bit of embarrassed guilt, "When that happens to Buddy I usually hold his hand and stroke his hair, and he

settles right down. I had the impulse to do
the same for you just now . . . sorry . . ." She
colored quickly.

"Red becomes you," he said. "Actually, I
can't think of anything I'd like better right
now. No violent, energetic movement required.
I just have to lie here and let a good-looking
woman stroke my hair. Yeah, I like it."

She smiled; he tried to but became aware
of the cadenced throbbing overcoming his left
arm and shoulder.

"But I'd kill for a drink of water, first."

"I'll tell the nurse and see what I can find."

He felt utterly limp and exhausted, a dead
weight of organic material denting a bed that
threatened to smother him. He was reminded
of the way Wilton Knight had looked on his
deathbed. At the same time he kept his eyes
open so he could watch Maggie walk out of
the room with her typical haughty stride.

It would be quite pleasant to spend a few
calm days in her company, just relaxing,
talking. Escaping the sensation of rushing
headlong toward some ugly end at burnout
speed. But the image of Wilton Knight commanded his attention as well. The old million-
aire had been avenged, but vengeance was
not all he had required of Michael. Vengeance
was a simple conclusion, a balancing of scales
that was really a pendulum swing—because
the objects of a vendetta always came back to
haunt one, either in person or through operatives, descendants or allies. Knight must have

realized this. So revenge was not what he had needed of Michael.

Michael tried to ponder just what it was Wilton Knight had in mind as he died in his mansion, grasping the hand of a stranger.

Maggie returned with a nurse in tow and handed him a paper cup filled with water. Simple water had never tasted so good, so invigorating.

He was alive. He had survived. Again.

"I just need to check your vital signs," said the nurse. "Welcome back."

"So tell me everything I need to know about myself," said Michael.

She wound a blood-pressure cuff around his right biceps. "Well, you've been asleep for nearly twenty-four hours, and we've been sliding as much glucose and plasma into you as we can get away with charging for." In a more serious tone she said, "You got rid of a lot of blood, you know."

"Devon's going to kill me for getting it all over his brand-new car, I know."

"By now you've noticed the bandages," she continued. "We got you plugged up, but do us a favor—no pumping iron for a while, huh? The bullet tore into your muscle tissue and stopped against the bone. Knocked out a chip that we had to remove. Your arm's going to be stiff and sore for a week or two, but you'll regain flexibility gradually. In a few days you'll start squeezing the rubber ball; you know how that works, right?"

Michael nodded.

"Officially you're mobile, but the doc has recommended you camp out right here for at least another day."

"I'd love to," said Michael. "But Devon may have other plans for me."

"I met him," Maggie put forth. "Such a distinguished-looking man. Eyes that really put you on the spot. He has an absentminded kind of refinement about him. I love his accent."

"Yeah, Devon's a real lady-killer," Michael joked. "Did you two get acquainted? Drag all my dirty secrets out and cackle over them?"

"Not actually. He seemed somewhat relieved that I was willing to stay and sit watch on you here at the hospital. He was quite anxious to examine the car, though."

"That sounds more like Devon."

Maggie dragged one of the visitor chairs over to Michael's bedside as the nurse left the private room to do other tasks. "He also had to do some things attendant to the authorities taking Tanya and the others into custody. He spent most of yesterday talking with all kinds of humorless government types."

"I think *procedure* will be his undoing." They both laughed.

She had his hand in hers again. "Tanya has a lot of evidence against her," she said. "They've pegged her as the ringleader."

"Good."

"She'll probably do a pretty long stretch in prison—that is, if she ever gets out of the intensive care ward." Maggie's eyes lowered.

"Don't pity her, Maggie," said Michael. "Not now. Remember all the people she's victimized, quite without any feeling whatsoever."

"I was thinking about Philip," she said. "And her. And how the thing I despise most is how violence and ugliness are sometimes the only way you can set things right. A lot of people just aren't capable of that sort of thing, Michael ... and they're fated to be life's big victims. Unless somebody like you comes along."

"Maggie, I'm not looking for gratitude," he said.

"I know, I know. But you've got mine anyway, whether you were in the market for it or not."

With forced lightness he said, "I think Devon's created a new employment category for me—White Knight."

"God, what an awful pun," she said. "You mean you're going to do this for a *living?* Butting into other people's disasters and spending every weekend in the hospital, healing?"

"I don't know." He truly did not.

"Well, I don't know how I'm going to keep Buddy thrilled after you go." She removed her hand from his and began to wring her own together.

"I'd keep him," Michael said. "Buddy's a pretty good kid."

"You know what I mean. He needs a man around, a father figure. You know it, I know it and anybody can see it."

He looked at her. "But your problem isn't Buddy," he noticed. "It's you."

She nodded. "Uh-huh." She wiped briefly at her eyes. "I thought I could just stay numb, you know? Just be tough and keep moving on through life and not caring . . ."

"And not looking?"

"Stupid, right?" She met his eyes but looked away too quickly. "Here I had a prime candidate right under my nose and I chased him away. Gave him a beer bath and rammed his car within twelve hours of our first hello."

"Wait a minute," Michael said. "I'm not Superman. I'm not just going to fly off into the sunset and never be heard from again."

"But you have to leave, right?"

"Not today. Today I'm not moving from this bed. And I'll be back to see you as soon as I can manage. You can tell Buddy that's a promise from me."

"You mean it?"

"Of course. But my business isn't finished, not yet. It doesn't end with Tanya, and it has to do with Devon and another man you don't know. Several men, actually." He thought of his past partners, of Muntzy, of Wilton Knight. "They're all dead. One of them used to be me."

"What do you mean?" said Maggie. "Sounds *ominous*." The tears were gone from her eyes.

"We've got all afternoon," he said. "Pull that chair a little bit closer. I've got a little story to tell you. . . ."

* * *

Devon's face was a caricature of exasperated outrage. He smacked a hand on KITT's dashboard. "Only *you* could have put a dent in this machine!" he said to Michael.

Devon was driving; Michael, safely installed in the passenger seat, was watching the scenery zoom past.

"He really didn't do it on purpose," KITT said. It did not help.

"You said this was a test run, right? Well, I pushed your little invention to the limit and it got a little scratched, that's it. Don't blow a gasket, Devon."

They were bound for the municipal airstrip where all the action had taken place several days earlier.

Silence settled between them for a few miles, then Michael said, "So when do I get the car back, Devon? I mean, how long will it take for you to check it up and fix it?"

"Yes, I'd be interested in the answer to that one," added KITT.

Devon looked at Michael as though he were examining a bacterium through a microscope. "Who said anything about you getting the car back?"

"It's my car, Devon. Remember?"

"Mr. Knight is in possession of the registration, Mr. Devon," KITT put in respectfully. *"If you'll check his driver's license, which you helped to supply in the first place, you'll find that—"*

"Enough!" said Devon. KITT fell silent. To Michael he said, "We'll have to have a little discussion about just who owns this machine, Mr. Kni—er, Michael."

Michael could not suppress a laugh at Devon's slip.

Parked next to the waiting Knight 2000 jet, which was warming up on the runway, was a long silver semi with the Knight Industries logo emblazoned on both sides of the box.

"Don't tell me," said Michael. "Now you've invented a truck that can survive a head-on collision with another truck."

Devon ignored the gibe, parking KITT in a position to drive up the auto ramp and into the body of the truck trailer. Inside the box Michael could see electronic equipment crowded together and winking on and off importantly. "This is KITT's home away from home," Devon said. "A mobile maintenance facility, completely self-contained and equipped."

"You mean for tune-ups, or something?"

"Roughly. Shall we go?" He indicated the waiting jet.

"Why don't you just let KITT drive himself back to the estate?" said Michael, but Devon ignored that, too. Michael had to trot to catch up with him as he made for the jet ramp.

Michael found himself continually glancing back at the car as he and Devon walked toward the jet. Strangely, he did not feel right leaving KITT behind.

"Don't worry," said Devon. "The truck will take KITT back to the estate."

Michael looked again and saw a svelte young woman with a captivating mass of dark brown hair step down from the truck cab. She was wearing close-fitting Knight Industries white coveralls that showed off her figure, and quite casually she drove KITT up the auto ramp and into the trailer.

"Is *that* one of the mechanics?" Michael asked, clearly surprised.

"Bonnie is like KITT's stepmother," Devon said. "You'll meet her later. That is, if you're still with us after you hear what I have to say."

Michael stalled at the bottom step of the jet's ramp, still looking back. The woman in the coveralls sealed the rear doors of the truck, hopped back into the cab and turned over the powerful semi engine.

"She doesn't look like anybody's mommy," Michael said.

As the Knight 2000 jet cut through the sky, Michael poured himself a glass of white wine from a chilled decanter. He liked to affect the habit of taking a small libation whenever he flew.

Devon was seated in one of the plane's leather swivel chairs, glancing with distaste over some documents he had withdrawn from his briefcase. Michael guessed that they were legal red tape having to do with the signing and sealing of Tanya and her cronies.

"Well now," Michael began. "If my job was done, I don't think I'd be this far up in the air." He had Devon's attention now, but the scientist merely raised his eyebrows, saying nothing. "Why don't we start with the car, Devon? What about it?"

Devon removed his glasses and rubbed his eyes. "Michael. Now that Wilton Knight is dead I have an ethical obligation to continue his work, to try and realize his personal dream. You, on the other hand, are under no such obligation. Your options are still quite open. I suppose I've been discourteous and unfair to you in that regard; that does not really concern me. You see—"

"Don't worry about it, Devon. You are forgetting something, though."

"What might that be?" He put his papers away.

"That Wilton Knight wanted me for whatever scheme he had in mind when he died. The 'great fight' he spoke of on his deathbed. The one he wanted *me* to lead. He said to me, 'You're the man who can make a difference, if you'll accept my legacy.'"

"I'm surprised you remember his exact words," said Devon.

"What's it all about, Devon? His 'legacy,' I mean."

"He wanted you to rid the world of Tanya and her friends, of course. I thought you would not be interested in the rest. Frankly, I thought that Wilton Knight's aspiration would bore someone like you to tears."

"Let's find out," Michael encouarged. "I mean, neither one of us is going to step out of the plane even if it *is* that outrageous."

Devon rose and helped himself to a glass of

wine. "It's merely a sort of . . . ah, insignifi-
cant foundation . . . we came up with an acronym for it—FLAG—but that's not important
right now."

"A foundation? You mean like a museum?"

"No. A private organization, devoted to
justice, to law. Sounds rather like the things
one sees in the comic books. But it's realisti-
cally grounded. Mostly paperwork, really. The
major portion of our activities involves in-
depth legal research, intercession in matters
of law along the lines of what the American
Civil Liberties Union does, class action suits.
But the seminal idea behind all the paperwork
is a kind of self-government, one that helps to
restore the concept of free will, replacing the
sense of predestination by which most people
live."

"The concept of free will," Michael said.
"That sounds closer to the Wilton Knight I
spoke with. And in a manner of speaking, I
spent a lot of time in the law business. In
Southeast Asia we were just playing interna-
tional policeman. I was a uniformed cop, a
representative of the enforcement arm of law.
Then a detective. What did Wilton Knight
want with a street cop?"

"Well apart from our research and intervention activities, which, as you've gathered, in-
volve the theoretical aspects and applications
of the law, Wilton Knight also felt that certain unjust situations—cases where there is a
clear wrongdoing or victimization, but no legal way to correct it in a courtroom or Senate

hearing—might be correctable only by direct action. If you're mugged in an alleyway you don't have time to argue ethics; direct action provides the only feasible solution. Our pilot program was to consist of one car. And one man capable of such individual action."

"*That's* why you didn't just override and take control of KITT when I was out there on the road, fighting the trucks and the Com Tron helicopter!" Michael realized. "You were testing *me* as well as that damned car!"

"As per Wilton Knight's orders," said Devon.

"I don't believe this!" Michael shouted. "I was bleeding to death, you could've saved me and you didn't lift a finger! Some philanthropist you are, Devon! Devoted to helping people? You'd've let me die out there."

"Lower your voice, Michael," Devon said with fatherly sternness. "You did not want my help, if you'll recall. You didn't even want KITT's assistance. Your exact words, if I recall, were 'I'm not relinquishing anything.' You refused to allow us to help you, or interfere. That very obstinacy on your part proves Wilton Knight's contention that you are singularly well qualified to 'go it alone,' as he put it to me once. You're a maverick."

Michael settled down. "This organization . . . you're talking about a bunch of people who intercede regardless of what the law says, is that correct? You feel that although you may not do what's legal, you do what's right."

"We haven't broken the law," said Devon.

"A street cop would argue that point with

you, Devon," Michael said as he thought of all the misdemeanors he'd committed while behind KITT's wheel. Just the speeding violations alone would have used up several ticket books. "You think you're above the law."

"There's a subtle difference," insisted Devon. "Our enemies are criminal types like Tanya who *operate* virtually above the law. Normal legal checks and balances can't touch them. We're after the Tanyas of the world."

"And sometimes you have to stretch the limits of the law to catch them. Yeah, I sure know how *that* works. We didn't actually *break* the law in setting up a lot of our 'sting' operations, but sometimes we had to bend it a little."

"Good laws are resilient," said Devon. "But to actually implement the FLAG pilot program we needed the man. The car we developed ourselves."

"What's the matter, Devon, didn't I pass the test?"

"That's not the point. I'm coming to realize that it would be absurd to expect any person to commit himself to the extreme required by Wilton Knight's ideal. Why, this one misadventure alone nearly cost you your life, and us the car!"

"Devon," said Michael sarcastically, "I didn't know you cared."

"The *point*," Devon persisted, "is that to expect any man or woman to do this sort of thing with any regularity would be asinine."

He folded his arms. "There are just too many risks involved."

"How do you know?" said Michael. "I mean, you don't really, now, do you? The only way to examine the efficacy of the program would be to see how it holds up in actual practice. And the only way to do that would be for me to go ahead and get involved in your pilot program, which is what Wilton Knight wanted all along."

"You wouldn't submit yourself to that." Devon sulked. "Just look at you."

"Now wait a minute. You're assuming I can just choose to opt out. But why can't I be as committed to an ideal as you—and you're committed to Wilton Knight's ideal. You *shared* it. Consider this, Devon: all my life I've been banging my head trying to take on criminals of one type or another who've always had the upper hand for the very kinds of legal reasons you've described. But now, here you and Wilton Knight come along and offer me a free hand to work as a—a maverick, you said. You hand me the world's most incredible car, and you back up the offer with the resources and finances of the Knight Foundation. What better chance could I get to actually be effective against such criminals, *and* at the same time vindicate Wilton Knight's idea that a single person could make a difference in the world. On top of it all, although I work alone, you're involved in each case— that's the teamwork you're always crowing

about. We both get what we want." He drained
off his glass and refilled it from the carafe.

"But why should someone like you choose
such a path at all? And what do you mean by
saying *I* assume you have a choice? Don't
you? Aren't you likely to walk away from this
place as soon as it lands and go back to arrest-
ing ruffians in the streets?"

"Because of two things, Devon. Wilton
Knight's dream makes a lot of sense to me.
Not the same way it does to you, granted. But
I believe in it. And I owe Milton Knight my
life, don't I? He died believing I accepted his
offer, didn't he? What kind of man am I, according to you, Devon? What kind would I
have to be in order to betray Wilton Knight
that way? That makes me no different from
Tanya!"

"You seem to be quite the ambitious loner,"
said Devon.

"And this opportunity is a loner's dream!"
Michael shrugged. "Look. I don't think you
and I are *ever* going to be in complete agreement on anything, Devon. But you're straight
and you're honest—"

"Gracious of you to say so." For someone
with no obvious funnybone, Devon could turn
acidly sardonic with pretty good comic timing.

"You know I'm the man Wilton Knight
wanted."

"Yes, in that particular area I *did* have no
choice."

"That sounds like what you were saying in
the car," Michael remembered. "About KITT's

programming. You got him to clam up as he was about to tell me something—when I claimed he could read my mind and you said that was silly."

"Yes, well . . ." Devon hemmed and hawed a bit, and it pleased Michael to see him off balance for a change. "It's just another aspect of the whole pilot program. Experimental."

"What is it, Devon? Come on."

"It's just that . . . Dr. Miles and I took pains to program KITT's machine personality for maximum interface value with the pilot-program driver—in this case, you. As the seat and dashboard are customized to your physical shape, so is the 'personality' of the micro-processor in conformity to your psychological profile." Devon's fist closed. "I'm sure you've noticed that it has started talking back to me! That's your fault, I believe."

Michael could not keep from laughing. "You mean I'm a bad influence on your car and I'm making it *misbehave?*"

"Bonnie will no doubt compensate for that little . . . er, malfunction."

"Devon, I think you just built it much better than you thought you did." He leaned against the bar. "You mean to say that my psychological profile says that a crazy Boston accent is the ideal voice for my robot pal?"

"Actually, KITT was originally designed with a woman's voice. In your case that would be—" Devon shuddered. "Disastrous."

"Why does it call you 'Mr. Devon'? Your

last name is Miles, isn't it? Same as the surgeon who did my face?"

"We are *not* related," Devon said icily. "I programmed in that aspect myself. It provides familiarity within a working relationship."

"I think I get it," said Michael. "The same reason why it stopped calling me 'Mr. Knight' and started calling me 'Michael.' "

"Exactly. The car *learns*—after a fashion— and its capacity grows according to what is most useful and least wasteful."

"But ... 'Mr. Devon'?" Michael thought about it for a minute. "I think the reason you were so irritated a moment ago is that you have some kind of daddy complex ... and you're afraid of me corrupting your child's personality."

Devon snorted. "That's neither here nor there. I was afraid your personality might bring you to the conclusions you've reached about the FLAG pilot program ... and the limits of my dedication to Wilton Knight. He was not only my employer,"

"You two were fast friends despite your constant bickering," said Michael. "Anybody could see it."

"Rather like you and KITT, now."

"Well, like *all* of us, Devon. The team—right? According to Wilton Knight's dictates, you've got no choice about me until I decide to leave. I'm sticking."

Devon nodded. "I was afraid of that, too."

Then he added, after waiting a beat, "That is, when we first started."

"You know, if one of you had told me all about this whole plan before, I might've been more responsive."

"You weren't *receptive* enough to be responsive."

"You mean it wasn't in the cards?"

"Wasn't in the psychological profile," Devon said, and reluctantly they both laughed together. "I think you're where you're supposed to be, now. Lord help us all."

Michael rose from his seat. "Bad attitude, Devon. No team spirit. Come on." He raised his glass. "Let's drink to—"

Devon interrupted. "To Wilton Knight's dream." He lifted his own glass.

"And to our future. Whoever it takes us up against, and wherever it takes us to."

"Sounds reasonable enough," said Devon. "You realize, of course, that in doing this we run the risk of being in complete agreement for once."

Michael nodded. "I'll take the chance. I'm as big a gambler as you."

"I beg your pardon. Me, a gambler?" His glass hesitated in his hand.

"Right. You gambled on me, didn't you?"

"Against my will. But I won, didn't I?"

"Looks like we both did. Here's to it." They clinked glasses in a toast and drained them off.

Michael resumed his seat across from Devon's. "Now I guess it's time for us to discuss the FLAG program in detail."

Devon nodded affirmatively, and reached again for his briefcase.

Alone in the sky, the Knight 2000 jet continued on its eastern course, moving toward home.